WATER

WATER

✦

H.E. TAYLOR

thistledown press

Library and Archives Canada Cataloguing in Publication

Taylor, H. E. (Harvey E.), 1948-
Water / H.E. Taylor.

ISBN 978-1-897235-23-2

I. Title.
PS8639.A948W38 2007   C813'.6   C2007-901610-3

Cover illustration by Philip Brogden
Cover and book design by Jackie Forrie
Typeset by Thistledown Press
Printed and bound in Canada by Marquis Book Printing Inc.

Thistledown Press Ltd.
633 Main Street
Saskatoon, Saskatchewan, S7H 0J8
www.thistledownpress.com

Canada Council   Conseil des Arts
for the Arts   du Canada

Canadian   Patrimoine
Heritage   canadien

We acknowledge the support of the Canada Council for the Arts, the Saskatchewan Arts Board, and the Government of Canada through the Book Publishing Industry Development Program for our publishing program.

Acknowledgements

I would like to thank Dr. Jill Tarter for her permission to quote the statement regarding the Drake Equation. I would also like to thank Dr. Michael Novacek, Dr. Norman Myers, Dr. Andrew Knoll and Elsa E. Cleland for their kind permission to quote their respective abstracts as chapter headings. My thanks also go to the PNAS editors who allowed their abstracts to be used. The complete references are in the footnotes. Further, I would like to thank the Dylan Thomas estate for their permission to use the poem title 'And death shall have no dominion.' In addition I would like to thank the Corydon Group —Ahniko, Louella, Gloria and Rick, for their many useful and insightful comments. The list would not be complete without thanking my editors, Al Forrie and R.P. MacIntyre who dealt with both me and my fractured language with equal grace.

for the Survivors

Contents

Intro

The Drake Equation
"Formulated by Dr. Frank Drake while drawing up an agenda for a SETI meeting in 1961, the Drake Equation was the first quantitative formulation of the probability of detecting extraterrestrial intelligence. The statement of the equation is:

$N = R f_p n_e f_l f_i f_c L$

Where:
N is the number of detectable civilizations in space,
R is the rate of star formation,
f_p is the fraction of stars that form planets,
n_e is the fraction of those planets hospitable to life,
f_l is the fraction of those planets where life actually emerges,
f_i is the fraction of planets where intelligent life evolves,
f_c is the fraction of planets with intelligent creatures capable of interstellar communication, and finally
L is the length of time that such a civilization remains detectable. Arguments regarding the specific values of various terms have continued unabated ever since."

— Encyclopedia Solaris [2646 OT Edition]

✦

SHE WOKE UP KNOWING WHAT SHE was and why, not where, when or who. She was an organ of the colony, a simulacra of a human, crafted by the ancient matrix. Travelling at two-thirds the speed of light toward the planet far ahead, she was a Human Contact Agent, an HCA, designed to facilitate understanding of the aliens. As for who she was, individuality was not practiced in the colony. The vast and complex symphonies of molecular intention by which the corporate intelligence communicated obviated unique identity. There were no individuals. There was only the Communion.

Aggregated over millions of years from thousands of planets, the quadrillions of cells constituting the colony shared identical DNA-like material. To create separate organisms, such as the HCA, the Communion activated only a subset of the total genome. Unlike the bulk of the colony, immediate pheromonal and electrochemical signalling were denied the HCA. To communicate, she had to impress meaning on sonic modulations. She had a mouth and ears. She had to talk and listen, exactly as did the noisy ones and that was problematic.

Saturated with the outlines of their languages, all that had been recorded from the planet ahead, she had much data, but very little knowledge. Many words were puzzling. There was no context for understanding. She was to study Earth, as the inhabitants called it, in order — her thoughts were more like listening to a recording than thinking — in order that the biospheric entities might be known — the meaning was not clear — in order that the biospheric entities might be incorporated. She recognized the imprint of the Communion in her programmed thoughts and did not question. Clarity would arise.

The HCA opened her eyes. Lying on a soft table in a room that appeared to be an amalgam of an operating theatre and an arboretum full of plants, she knew this seamless integration of biology and machine was all alive. The exterior shell and the interior compartments of the ship were also organs of the colony. She felt facial muscles moving in expressive patterns. In a hovering mirror she saw her silver-skinned, dark-eyed reflection, saw that in spite of her human shape, she retained the lithe grace of the Communion.

Above her stood another humaniform creature — bipedal, with a single head, two eyes, no nose, a mouth. Slight silvery stubs protruded on the side of the head where there should have been ears. A silver translation device in the creature's right hand said, "I am your Liaison ... "

As soon as she saw the electrochemical interface, the HCA realized the Liaison was effectively another layer of isolation to protect the colony. This information was not in her programming. "How far until. . . . she started to ask.

The Liaison silenced her and continued recording. "The probability is high this version of Human Contact Agent will function within specified norms."

She could not help but wonder how many other Liaisons were talking to how many other HCAs throughout the colony ship?

"Now, to respond to the implanted question." The Liaison lowered the shiny tube. "The ship will not reach the planet for gigachrons." A holodisplay of the galaxy popped into the air between them, the flight path of the ship marked in red. "And it is megachrons yet before deceleration begins." The HCA studied the display. "Rest now, and let the implanted curiosities grow in your mind. There is much to learn."

✦

Around the Earth, expanding spheres of electromagnetic radiation advertise the presence of humans. The Communion recorded, analyzed and decoded all it could for the HCA to experience. With the passing of megachrons, the HCA came to realize humans used proper names, and she started calling herself Xyala. The Liaison regarded this development with some alarm, as something akin to going native, but took no discernible action. The Liaison could never comprehend the purpose of the pronoun "I" — the notion of an abstract individual was simply too bizarre. Finally, Xyala decided not to tax the creature with the linguistic pattern. Some things about the humans only she would ever truly understand.

Xyala lived with the human data, immersing herself in the recordings from the distant planet. She wanted to experience as much as possible about the target species. This was her basic imperative, her reason for existence, which she naturally found interesting and fun. Humans were crude. The creatures bore the imprint of a troubled evolution. They had only recently mastered fusion, and worse, they were divided in some incomprehensible way. They never seemed to learn. They kept repeating the same mistakes. A reflexive activity called laughter utterly baffled her — and the mechanical noise they called music was eccentric beyond belief. Sometimes the alienness simply overwhelmed her. How could she ever hope to encompass such exotic strangeness?

The huge ship was coming up to the turnaround point when in the middle of analyzing the phenomena called religion, the HCA received an unscheduled visit. Blunt and to the point, the Liaison said, "All radio signals from the planet have ceased."

"What does that mean? What happened? Have they detected us? What have they done?" The questions tumbled out of Xyala and the Liaison regarded her with something resembling a mother's pride. Behind her questions, Xyala was wondering would the Communion now dissolve her? Was her task complete? She knew the concern was an aberration induced by her isolation, but she was powerless before the emotional imperative.

The Liaison strolled in front of a wall-sized video display showing ocean dotted by a chain of islands and covered by wispy cloud. "Find out what happened. Begin with the latest signals. The historical data can wait. In the meantime, be aware that the Communion will not decelerate immediately. Another source of artificial electromagnetic radiation lies a couple hundred light megachrons almost directly ahead. It seems to be another human cluster."

The Liaison was oblivious to Xyala's turmoil. If she said nothing, the Liaison would not even know her alien facial expressions could convey information. The Liaison continued, "There is a need to know what happened and why. Program a probe to collect high-quality data from the planet."

A wave of relief swept over Xyala. The Liaison was also oblivious to her reaction. It continued studying the planet displayed on the large wall panel and remarked, "Why is it called Earth, when it is mostly Water?"

Beginnings

"You can make guesses on all the factors in the Drake Equation, and, to within astronomical accuracy, that is to within a couple of orders of magnitude, right, the equation reduces to $N = L$. That is the Number of technological civilizations that we can communicate with in the galaxy is equal numerically to their Longevity in years. Now you tell me. How long does a technological civilization live?"

— Dr. Jill Tarter

◆

WE ARE THE PEOPLE. We live as we have always done, by the grace of the sun, on the bounty of the earth, because we are worthy. Since the animals left us, many of the ancient ways no longer apply. When the plants died, we had to adapt new ways. No longer does the great horned owl call our name; no longer do the caribou roam. The Old Ones are only a memory, but their works remain. The Ultras and the Machines remain, but we are the People.

Although we came from many lands, and although we were very different, the mutant and the lucky, we joined together. When it became clear there were no others, we knew we had to work together or die. We came together in the Big Sky Lodge and began to build. We knew the way of the small machines. In time, a few plants and animals returned. Far to the east, the Water Lodge did much the same. It is simple self-governance.

Life is different when you look ahead a thousand years, or ten thousand. We evolved a loose structure born of basic common law and Metis tradition, molded by the circumstances. We could not trust any plan, for who knows what the future might bring. We put our trust in people. We adapted the word "tribe" to indicate the nature and essence of an individual. And we adapted the word "work" to mean the tasks one assumes in life. A person is known by their tribe and their work. Of all the billions before the fall, we are not many, a few thousand, and for all that, we are no longer quite human. We do not die easily.

The dream changed shape. The dreamer spoke.

I am Wilhemina Featherstone, but I hate that name, so everybody calls me Billie. My tribe is hunter and my work is guarding the People. I roam the border of the southern wastes — watching for danger, looking for opportunity. I roam because I hear the call of the road and because I will never be a mother. For a time, after I came to understand, I could not accept that hard fact. That was several lifetimes ago. I played at sex with many men — to no avail. The men of the village lost interest. As far as they were concerned, I was broken, a toy to be played with, not anyone that mattered. They want children — even if most of them are not whole. Damaged by radiation, by chemicals, by the biowar viruses, broken and half-human, condemned to the Mission though their progeny may be, they keep trying — but not with me. Not with me.

I left them and I wandered. The village people could say what they liked. I let it go. I would guard them all for the ones I loved. I became Billie the Ranger. I grew to love the desert as a child loves fire. The sun, the wind and the still, still land. It creeps into my heart and I find myself in the silence — wide-open spaces where I can see right to the horizon.

I was sitting with some people in a kitchen when this woman walked up. An earlier generation would have taken one look and said Metis. She had an athletic, self-contained look about her — tall and broad-shouldered. With short sunburnt ruddy brown hair, and two bright laughing eyes set in a smooth skinned, fine featured, almost tiny face, she looked down at me. She wore simple clothes, dungarees and a work shirt. There was an air about her. She was almost bashful, with a quiet self-confidence and something I could not put my finger on. She kept smiling at me with an odd expression. Then I realized —she was me.

Her heart pounding, Billie awoke with a start. She was shaking. She wrapped her arms around herself listening to the still and quiet night. Why had the ancestors spoken to her? The air was thick and heavy with humidity. Silence reigned. She listened until her heart slowed down, then sighed abruptly and stood. It was her last night in her own bed until next winter and she had not slept well. She resolved to talk to Finian about the dream and distracted herself by starting her day.

She stumbled into the washroom and performed her morning ablutions perfunctorily in a half-light. In the kitchen she turned on a low lamp and warmed some leftover tea. Back in the darkness of the front room, she padded over to the window, a mug of tea in her hand, and sat regarding the full moon. It was smooth. The lighter sections appeared almost polished. She was not old enough to remember the Day with Two Suns, but she had seen the old pictures. She knew how the moon used to look. A lunar surface sparkling with light from every dome — the home of millions. And now it was billiard-ball smooth.

The man in the moon was gone with the Fusion War and so were the Lunies.

Billie mused on the word — the Lunies, the loonies. It was funny-strange how a group of people could take a derogatory term like that and turn it into a badge of honour. It was like Finian. If you asked him, he would tell you his tribe was freak and his work knowledge. Billie did not know just what to think of that declaration, but she recognized that Finian used the word freak as a badge of honour in the same way the moon folk had called themselves Lunies.

"And you, my silver sister," Billie held her mug of tea up to the moon, as if in a toast, "what fools do you think these mortals be?" She sipped a smile.

It was the hour before dawn. Everything was ready for her patrol. She had only to dress and go. Her jeans and shirt were waiting. In mid-morning she would see Finian and be off. Finian, notoriously, did not keep hunter's time, or farmer's time either for that matter, and she would have to wait for him to be mobile. He was getting old again. Billie sat and watched the moon, thinking of her friend.

Among the chronologically oldest of Big Sky, Finian had come to the People with a knowledge of nanoprogramming in the early days. Before the few plants that survived had propagated and begun to grow again, before the dog and the rat returned, when it had seemed for a while that every living thing might die, it was Finian's skill and knowledge which had crafted the foodstuffs, the sugars and proteins, the vitamins and starches that the people needed. By that time, very little old food remained to use as a template. The tiny molecular machines could make anything, but only if they had the correct instructions. Finian had worked from theory, not by duplication. Billie chuckled. There were still some old-timers who ribbed Finian about the tasteless grey paste he had cranked out to keep them alive. In joking gratitude they would call him "cookie" or "chef" and everyone would laugh.

As it turned out, Finian never did get up. He was sick in bed. It was almost noon when Piotr, his apprentice, met Billie at the door. He was worried and annoyed. "The old man is in one hell of a mood," Piotr hissed in Billie's ear as she entered the den where Finian lay.

"What on earth have you done to poor Piotr?" she asked.

"Oh Billie. Good. I'm glad you stopped by," he replied, with no apparent intention of answering her question. "Come in and have some tea. There's toast as well." He lay propped up on pillows under a pile a blankets on a small soft bench to one side of the room. A shock of white hair hovered over two burning eyes in a deeply lined face.

"I'll have some toast, but I'm already tea to the eyebrows from all I drank waiting for you this morning." His only reply was a grunt.

No sooner had Billie sat down than Piotr was at the door again. "Excuse me Finian, but Slivers from Three Islands is here. He says he needs an impellor and a bearing mount for his deep-water pump." Piotr did not enter the room, but stood respectfully or fearfully, Billie could not tell which, at the door. "Oh yes, and he says he will need a three-room instahouse for his oldest son, who is getting to be too big for his britches." Piotr finished reciting his clearly memorized request and waited.

"Hmmm. An impellor — that's just iron, nickel and magnesium. You know where the templates are. Draw materials and go ahead and crank it."

Billie noticed the boy's eyes light up. "We'll have to talk about the instahouse. There may be more to that than meets the ear." Piotr nodded and was quickly gone.

"He likes what he is doing anyway," said Billie, "and that counts for something." Finian did not reply. They sat in silence, savouring their moment, sipping tea and eating toast. Billie had come to appreciate those, like Finian, who heard the roar of silence and were not afraid. A minute, five minutes later, she put her cup down.

"I'm heading out today. I wanted to check if you need anything," Billie said.

"The inventory is over there." Finian gestured to a smart wall, which displayed a list of materials when Billie touched it. "I got the list ready for you knowing you would be around."

Billie scrolled the list up and down reading at eye level. The sorted inventory was accompanied by stock on hand and rate of usage figures which made the priorities clear.

"The main thing we need is titanium. There are a couple of agrobots I cannot rebuild properly because I have none now. I've had to substitute, not always effectively."

Billie nodded. Finian was their best nanoprogrammer and if he could not get a substitute working well, then likely nobody could. Finian kept the stockpile of elements and material needed for his work in the warehouse and yard behind the house. Billie looked out the window at the yard. Her eyes rose to the horizon and she remembered her dream. She and Finian got along well, especially when he was in his older aspect. He was almost like a father at such times. In another ten or fifteen years, he would be younger than her again. And then he would be just another silly man. She smiled to herself and turned back to Finian.

"I had a dream. The grandfathers spoke to me."

"Yes?" They locked eyes. He wasn't making this any easier for her.

"It frightened me. Why would they talk to me?"

"What did they say?"

"They spoke of the People and the land. Then I met myself and woke up."

Finian smiled. "Yes. That is the kind of trick they enjoy." He sipped his tea.

Billie looked so distraught, he was moved to say, "The only time the ancestors spoke to me was when my life was changing. What is your tribe?"

"Hunter."

"And what is your work?"

"Guarding the People."

"What is changing for you?"

"Nothing as far as I know."

"Then we will have to wait and see."

Billie sighed and shook herself. "And how are you, old friend?" she asked with sudden earnestness.

"Oh hell I'm fine. I get annoyed. There are so few born whole; so few interested in learning. I cannot teach a sense of play, a spirit of exploration, where true creativity begins. Piotr memorizes, but he does not think. Oh he is a good boy, but . . . "

Finian caught the uncomfortable look that flitted across Billie's face and coughed to change gears. "So now you are off again. Do you have all the crystals you need?"

Billie shook her head. "I could use some more Remove. Last fall I ran into a string of infestations in the west, if you recall, and used up most of mine."

Finian nodded. "Tell Piotr. I got him to crank a supply for you just last week."

Billie stood at the door looking back at Finian propped up under the comforters.

"Take care." "Take care." They said simultaneously and both broke into laughter.

Minutes later, with a supply of new Remove crystals in her pouch and a sense of anticipation rising in her spirits, Billie strode through the warehouse of elements, out through the hazardous materials beyond and into the open country to the south.

As Billie walked, she thought at first of practicalities. A leaving is always a time of considerations. You have to think what you will take and what you will leave behind. Inevitably you think of who you leave behind. Billie had made her rounds so many times, she scarcely had to think, but still she catalogued those few items she carried. She always travelled light and fast — some tools, some clothes, some food and nothing electronic — electronics in the desert tended to draw Ultras, and that was a grief she did not need. As she catalogued, she found herself thinking of her friends, her cousins — the faces of the people of the village drifted before her mind's eye. Her parents who had disappeared. Billie remembered how she had first become interested in Finian when she learned that the bright-eyed aelfscin creature had created Restart in the old days and simply neglected to inform his military masters.

Protecting these folks was a worthy thing to do, she thought as she walked. Even if, she had no illusions, she was not much protection — an advance warning, perhaps, an antenna for the People. Others patrolled closer to the villages, and later in the season, the desert would force her further north as well. Still the People would not be bothered by nanobugs. No surprises would come out of the southern badlands, and they would rarely think to wonder why. But then again, neither would they see the sun rise on a perfectly clear desert sky, thought Billie with a sigh.

Billie had walked only a couple of kilometres when a truck rumbled down the road from the village. She stuck out her thumb.

"Hello Billie" said the young man driving as she clambered into the cab. An odour of biogas permeated the vehicle. The fuel cells worked well, but the gas stank. Her nose wrinkled. She dropped her bag just in front of her seat. "You're lucky. I was just about to put it in auto and catch some sleep. Another kilometre and old Betsy" — he slapped the steering wheel — "would have just rolled right by you."

Billie did not know the driver by name, although she had seen him around. He introduced himself as Philby, and braggingly apologizing about a wild party last night, put the truck in autodrive and crawled into the sleep space at the back of the cab.

Billie watched the country roll by. She had some thousand kilometres to go, south by southeast, before the last farm — the Stirling place. Beyond that, the Last Bush was another five or six hundred kilometres. As she rode the transport south, she watched the country change.

In this district, it was mainly bush — all varieties of poplar. The evergreens had all disappeared in the biowar. From the ancient highway, Billie could see a wall of bush, with only the odd pocket of cleared and cultivated land. Not long before, this land had been muskeg and it took fifty years to make a centimetre of good black top soil, where the bacteria and subsoil insects survived.

In one field, agrobots were working beside the road. She wondered where the crucial titanium was in the semi-smart machine. Perhaps the disc blades; perhaps the skeleton. They were soon out of sight behind the speeding truck. The trees died down, smaller and paler, the further south they went.

The bush died out and only along waterways were there any trees. The only green was now the grass. It was idiosyncratic which plants had survived the extinction event. The genetech plants had been specifically targeted during the biowar. It was the gene sequences which happened not to be known which survived, or those old species with varied populations of mutant alleles — saskatoons, poplar, willow, rapeseed, millet, a variety of wild rice. Besides the plants, there was little else. A few insects, some inedible fungi had turned up; and of the animals, few remained, a couple of birds, the dog and rat. The species that survived tended to be generalists; animals that could live on anything. Among birds, it was the ones that did not migrate. Billie rode through the day, watching the land become drier. Bushland became prairie, and prairie became desert as they rolled south.

When the truck pulled into the sleepy little shipping station, Billie's luck held out and she was able to catch an autotruck to the Stirling place. There was no cab, so she jumped into the freight box. The last thing carried in the vehicle had apparently been soil, because a fine and lumpy black layer had dried and hardened to the metal. Everything that touched it turned black; her pants, her hands, her bag. She leaned back against the hard metal side and didn't worry about it.

The highway became road and the road became trail; the vehicle moved more and more slowly. It was better than walking, but just barely. The vehicle used infrared for night guidance, so Billie could see nothing after sunset. The moon was scant help. She spent an uncomfortable night being jostled around in the back of the truck.

It was mid-morning when the truck rolled into the Stirling yard and shut itself off. Billie stood up in the truck box and looked around. She was stiff and sore and she had slept very little. Surrounded by poplar trees, the house was built on a slight rise at the end of a long and fairly wide depression which the Stirlings irrigated with well water. It was a little island of green sheltered from the restless wind by the dip in the land. The trees were another layer of protection. The house's photovoltaic roof glistened in the sun.

These people did not lead an easy life. They lived by breeding dogs. Well, they called them dogs, but in fact they were coyotes, no more than a dozen generations from the wild. The domesticated canine breeds had all gone with the Old Ones. The dogs lived on rats, which were actually a cross between gophers and a type of lab rodent, the only genmod life form Billie knew to have survived the great die off. The Stirlings trapped the rats and bred the dogs. They did not use agrobots; they were of little use for rat or dog. It was a truncated and narrowly based ecology, which was inherently unstable and they knew it.

The yard was quiet in the hot morning sun. A wisp of smoke rose from the chimney. The voices of children playing by the back door drifted through the air. One of the children saw her and yelled. "Hey Billie!" An immediate commotion arose among the others. "It's Billie. It's Billie," the little girl shouted in glee, running across the farmyard. Two more bright smiling faces appeared and joined the race.

The backdoor of the house swung open and a female voice called, "Come on in!"

The children were all over her, wanting to be carried, wanting to be played with. The youngest girl's right eye was deformed. Her eyebrow dipped inward where it ought not to and the smaller-than-usual eye looked like it was pulled back into a knot by her temple. It did not slow her down in the least. Billie remembered her shock when she had first seen the infant, and Jeb Stirling had simply said, "If she dies, I will make another." The infant mortality rate was so high that nobody invested much emotion in the newborn. Ultimately, that was behind the custom of adult naming. The children would not be officially named until they came of age. The artificial retroviruses still in the environment from the biowar, made the nine month journey of the foetus hazardous in the extreme. The journey afterwards was no less dangerous. Those who did not have the required mutations died, plain and simple. The Stirlings had already lost several.

With a child on either shoulder, Billie stopped at the foot of the stairs to the back door. She squatted down and set the kids on the ground. The oldest girl who was making a valiant effort to carry Billie's shoulder bag, and was dragging it across the gravelly yard, suddenly let go shouting, "Me! Me!" and ran pell-mell towards Billie. She caught the child and straightened, tossing her shrieking up into the air.

"Me next," said the boy seriously, pulling at her shirt.

Jayne Stirling pushed the back door open with her shoulder again and stuck her head out. "You children go and feed the dogs. For heaven's sake let Billie be." The door slammed. Billie laughed. "Ah mom," said one and they were off, running and yelling toward the pens in the back. Billie scooped her bag from the ground, brushed off some of the dirt and opened the back door.

"Come in. Come in. Ah it's good to see you. Jeb is out trapping in west–thirty-nine. Come in and tell me all the news. I've been thinking you might be coming round this way about now." Jayne spoke over her shoulder.

The land was marked out in square kilometres, and Billie didn't know exactly where west-thirty-nine was, but she knew it was away. She blinked her eyes in the sudden dimness. The kitchen was a bustling affair with children's toys scattered on the floor beneath the large wooden table, hunting rifles on the wall, a pile of breakfast dishes waiting to be washed and the wonderful smell of baking bread filling the air. An evidently unused communication console sat in the corner covered with toys and tools.

"I'd give you a hug, but . . . " Jayne turned holding up two flour-coated hands. The flour was a mixture of wild rice and millet. Wheat was a thing of the past. She flopped a roll of dough over a flour-covered board, kneading and working it with her hands. "There's biscuits in the oven. Can you stay the night?"

Billie shook her head and said, "No. I don't think so. I want to get on the road soon." She knew these folk were glad to see her, they had so few visitors, but she was just passing by. She was not about to get comfortable. The day was young and she felt the road beckoning.

Jayne smiled in acknowledgement. She knew Billie's ways. "Ah well. I'll get a good meal into you anyway. Sit down. Take a load off your feet. I'll bet your backside is glad to be out of that truck."

Billie laughed. The thunder of children's footsteps banged on the back stairs. The youngest girl burst into the room and wormed her way onto Billie's lap. The oldest girl went directly to the front room. In a few seconds she came back holding a mason jar with something shiny in it.

"Billie look what I found." She held the jar out.

"Oh yes, I was going to mention that to you," said Jayne.

Billie put the girl back on the floor and took the jar. Inside was a dragonfly — a large dead dragonfly. She had only seen one in pictures and video in the village. She remembered being fascinated by how the insect used to float and dart. A perplexed look on her face, Billie looked at Jayne. Jayne paused and shrugged. With the badlands to the south and Machines to east and west, there was nowhere the dragonfly could have come from, few insects on which it could have lived — and yet there it was. Billie put the jar down thoughtfully.

For an hour, Jayne and Billie chatted while the children played underfoot. A battle royale erupted over a toy, tears were shed and one child was sent outside to water the rats. While she sat in the kitchen, the smell of baking worked wonders on Billie's appetite. The bannock and stew was simple and filling. Before Billie left, Jayne gave her a supply of dried dog meat and bannock. A small bag of biscuits and bread was "just for a treat," said Jayne with a grin. She knew they would not stay fresh long.

It was a well-fed and resolute Billie that trudged down the lane in early afternoon. She passed the Stirling windmills lazily churning in the light breeze. As the valley fell away and the sun beat down, Billie suddenly felt the heat. She pulled her carbon-fibre hat from her pack and fished for the snap-on sun shield. With a flap at the back to protect her neck and the graduated polarizing filters in place, a sensation of relief radiated from her eyes. Billie felt in her element. She would wear the hat the rest of the summer. It was important to dress sensibly; heatstroke was always a problem, particularly when water was scarce.

That evening, far to the south of the Stirling place, Billie passed the Ultra poles. She was now in Ultra territory. It was a mystery why, but for some reason, the Ultras never bothered people north of the poles. At least, not so far as anybody knew. There were occasional disappearances, like Billie's parents long ago, but nobody knew for sure what had happened. You heard the phrase "taken by Ultras" once in a while, but like so much to do with the Ultras, there were few hard facts and many stories. They were a mystery wrapped in the fear of the unknown. One hard fact, however, was that south of the poles, you were liable to run into Ultras anywhere. Electromagnetic signals would always draw them. That was why Billie travelled notech. The best that could be said for the Ultras was that they didn't care much about humans. And the worst, was that they were some kind of weird kidnappers, perhaps slavers. Billie's mentor, Jack, had simply disappeared in the southern desert. Others had come back with stories of being held for days unable to speak.

Unfortunately, the south was the place to find the old equipment and the refined metals needed by Finian's machines. And unfortunately, the nanobug infestations always came from the south carried by the wind. So it was a good thing stealth did not seem to come naturally to the Ultras. They used a noisy aircar that advertised its presence making avoidance possible.

As for the land itself, there was nothing ahead of her but sand and sun. Survival here in the near desert was a matter of water. Billie knew all the old farm wells. Over the years she had come to know this territory by heart. She made her way, day by day into the dryness, hiking from well to well. There was no hurry. She took her time and scouted out the land, becoming more cautious as she moved southward. If there were danger, she would find it. If she came across metal, Finian would get it.

The route she would follow over the course of the summer flashed through Billie's mind. She would swing southeast, following a zigzag line of wells, until she hit the Last Bush. The scraggly line of stunted willow followed a creek along the old riverbed. The water was on the surface now; later in the year she would have to dig. Beyond that mark, few wells survived. Some were bad; some were drifted in. She would trace a line across the south, past the Dead City, following the old water course as it arced towards the southwest wrapping around abandoned farms and the Mission. In the west, where the Last Bush approached the Machines, she would swing north, reprovision and then go back the other way, moving slightly further north each trip as the season and the dryness progressed. She would not see the village again until late next fall.

The days flowed by like a dream. Billie loved this land with a fierce and wild passion she could never explain. She walked in the wind, and at night, the wind walked in her dreams. The sun was her only companion.

When she was in the village, in the great lodge, she would talk about being out on the flat, where you can see forever, and people would laugh. It was well-meaning laughter. It was poor Billie with no children, poor Billie watching out for us, alone in the wild. They did not understand. The People treated her with respect, called her a Ranger, but they did not feel what she felt, did not see what she saw — except, perhaps, for Finian and Hannah.

Finian seemed to understand. He paid attention out of some calculation, Billie felt, perhaps because in some way he viewed her as a resource to be utilized effectively. She liked Finian, but his simple manner did not tell the whole story by any means. Perhaps, in fact, he viewed the whole matter differently. She was not entirely sure.

Hannah was another story. Hannah understood with her heart. Some species of the same fire that moved Billie, burned and blessed her veins. That was why she lived in the Mission, so far into the southern wastes. Billie thought of all the birth defects, the malformed and disabled children Hannah cared for and housed. And yes, she dared say it, loved. She wondered what moved the old woman to assume such a burden; could not imagine how anyone would do that. There! I am not any better than the village folk, she thought with a laugh.

On the horizon a group of buildings stood among collapsing sheds. She would have a fire tonight. Billie paused and pulled her vuscope out of her bag. She scanned the buildings, and then the surrounding countryside. Nothing moved. The well is just past that last barn, she thought.

Billie made camp in the darkening day. Sometime during the night, a strange bird flew overhead. The kree, kree call awakened her momentarily, dragged her from the shapeless depths and left a lingering curiosity. What manner of bird had that been and where had it come from? It was not a raven, not a sparrow, the only two birds Billie had ever seen alive. What was it? She dreamed of a floating and flitting dragonfly.

False dawn limned the northeast sky, when Billie arose from her troubled sleep. An image of the dragonfly hung yet in her mind. She decided to skip her morning meal, refilled her water and was soon headed out across the cool morning desert. Her mind roiled with the extinction. It troubled her thoughts like a great black dog that refused to go away. It was not that she missed the old world, she had never known any world other than her abbreviated version. She had seen the pictures, old video and holo records of fabulously baroque creatures — lions and giraffes, elephants and whales, cockatoos and kangaroos — all gone now. To Billie they were like a dream, a troubling dream of overwhelming force.

The world had been plundered, the countryside savaged, whole ecosystems destroyed. Then global warming had kicked in with a vengeance, the waters rose, the deserts grew and billions had to move or die. That necessity had triggered wars, chemical, biological, nuclear, then nano — the madness of a world culture that saw itself as something above and beyond nature, struggling in a trap of its own devise.

She had listened to the holos of old ecologists. Even though it is difficult for a creature that lives a hundred years, to see a thousand year long pattern of change, the Old Ones knew the extinction was happening. They knew there were too many people, but they couldn't do anything about it. Not many volunteered to be childless. There was food to be put on the table. There was too much money to be made.

The talk of money lost Billie. She had seen the old coins, listened to the stories, but had never felt the power, the compulsion of the old ways. The Big Sky folk lived what might be called a mixed economy. It was like a stratigraphic cut across several layers of history and social organization. They all coexisted, because when you don't know if you're going to live or die, you simply use what works. Some lived a not–so-simple, hunter-gatherer existence, while others farmed or ranched like the Stirlings, and yet others utilized the old tech. There was no currency. Barter and community were the extent of Billie's financial experience. She was a Ranger because the task needed to be done; she loved the land and it suited her nature. She was not paid. The very idea would have seemed not credible to her. If somebody had something you wanted, you bartered for it, or you made a copy. Nanotech made the concept of property fluid.

The old world was gone, but in another way it was still very much present. Little practical knowledge was lost; the old computer systems still ran. Enough of the old tech existed to be copied. It was a change of focus. The centre of gravity had moved, as Hannah had put it to Billie once. Those few inhabitants of the planet who remained, the humans, the Ultras, even the Machines — if you could call that living — were bound by the knowledge of that paroxysm. The extinction, the great death, the die off — it had many names — sometimes just the fall. No land animal over twenty kilograms except humans survived. As Hannah frequently said, we were not expelled from the garden, we destroyed it.

Humans crawled back from that abyss, knowing the edge would never again be far away. The golden age, the noble savage, the mythos of some perfect past disintegrated in the knowledge of what had been done, in the reality in which they found themselves. The past was accursed; the present a trial; the future an open question. What they might yet build, what they might yet come to understand, what they might yet become, depended simply upon what would grow. The dead dragonfly and the strange new bird flew through her meditation, tantalizing and intriguing her.

Billie wandered through the morning with her head full of dreams, her heart embroiled in the extinction. As the sun rose, so did the temperature. She stopped to remove a layer of clothes and have a drink. The countryside was crackling in the sunlight, stretching with the warmth.

Billie pulled her vuscope out of her bag and sat with her back against a dead poplar tree stump. The top of the big tree was broken off at about three metres. No sign that anything else had ever grown here remained beside the stump. She surveyed the country. No animal moved and no bird sang. To her surprise a ground wasp drawn by her water buzzed around and settled on the still damp lip of her water bottle. "Now you're a long way from home," she said. Billie watched it idly as it explored the surface of the sealed container.

She brought the vuscope to her eye again and happened to catch the sun glinting from an nano iridescent surface to her right. She gazed intently. It was small and moving. She decided to look a little closer. It looked like nanobugs. Nanobugs were old miltech. They had originally been created as surveillance devices and, according to Finian, if you had a gigahertz receiver, you could still pick up transmitted data. That imperative had never been lost. But whether it was something in the wars, or some nanohacker or what, the devices had become self-replicating and were out of control now. Luckily they were stupid, and reproduced slowly as nano went — slower than insects, for that matter. Still, it was better to get rid of them before the heat of the summer boosted their activity level.

Billie stopped about a hundred metres from the nest and watched the creatures with her vuscope. It was definitely bugs. Chuckling wryly, she felt in her pouch of nanotools. Finian had asked for titanium, and instead he was first going to get a dose of silicon. Oh well, at least he would know she was okay. She studied the swarming mass. It appeared the bugs had found an old computer centre. She knew there were other underground complexes near here and the bugs liked the highly refined silicon. They swarmed all over the rectilinear shapes protruding from the sandy soil.

With a crystal of Reclaim in one hand and a crystal of Remove in the other, she crept closer to the buzzing perimeter. The Remove was a variant of Reclaim aimed directly at the silicon creatures. Once triggered it radiated an infrared signature which would draw any bug within a hundred metres. Then the disassembly portion of the tool would come into play and the nanobugs would be disabled and taken apart, atom by atom. The material would be wrapped in a winged carbon shell, which would fly to Finian's warehouse of elements using sunlight energy. The only problem was Billie had to get the Remove into the middle of the nanobugs and they were moderately dangerous. If one landed on her, it might just decide it could use her elements and begin to replicate. That was why she had the Reclaim. Reclaim would not touch human cells, and if a bug landed on her, she could use it as a bug swatter.

Billie edged in to about ten metres from the churning mass and threw the crystal of Remove underhand into the middle. In five seconds, a loud, high-pitched whine pierced the air. The bugs all scrambled towards the crystal where a strange shimmer overtook them. Nanowar raged. The Remove neutralized and disassembled the nanobugs. Carbon was taken from the atmosphere and flying surfaces constructed. The energy of the sun was caught. Millions and millions of tiny winged shells encapsulated the elements of the creatures. Above the whirling centre, a plume of black dots spiralled and climbed, curving slowly towards the north. Hello Finian, thought Billie with a laugh. For thirty minutes, she watched the nest dissolve. Gradually stillness and silence returned.

Billie decided it would be best to get rid of the raw silicon, so when the Remove had finished its work, she cautiously approached the cavity where the bugs had nested. Unrecognizable stumps of ancient machinery jutted into the air. Evidently there was a lot more underground. Finian might get a lot more material than he wanted, she thought, but knew the Reclaim would move no more than about ten thousand kilograms, and he was always shunting materials around. Billie squeezed and scratched a ten second delay active containment crystal over the old stumps of machinery and moved quickly away. Again a swirl of black motes arose, arcing toward the north. With a rumble, the ground shook as manufactured materials were suddenly removed — dissolved and converted into flying motes. Sections of ground fell away. Dust and debris puffed up into the air. Billie scooted further out of the way.

Billie returned to the poplar tree where she had seen the wasp, and once again sat with her back to the stump surveying her domain. Stillness penetrated to the bone. She took a drink of water and sighed. The rest of the day she spent travelling in a slow spiral outwards from the cavity where the bugs had been. She stopped every once in a while and used her vuscope to look for more of the nanobugs.

As she searched, Billie found herself thinking about tools and machines. Her thought was drawn down an ineluctable line of logic. Every tool is an extension of a human modality, Finian had once told her. And it made sense as far as it went. Her vuscope was an extension of her eyes; the autotruck an extension of her feet. But there were machines, and there were machines. There were simple tools like the vuscope or the lever. And then there were the smart dumb machines like the agrobots some of the farmers used. They knew how to do some things well, but they didn't know why. "Idiot savant expert systems" Finian called them.

And then there were the wild machines, like the nanobugs, which were really more like insects as far as people were concerned. But there were also the smart wild ones — the Machines. People pronounced the word like it was capitalized. They were dangerous, but not hostile. It was more like they were indifferent, which was scarier in some ways. The Machines treated people like raw material. Anybody who strayed too near the Machines did not return.

Some of the older folks in Big Sky said the Machines used to be human once. There were few useful computer records of the creatures. But why would anyone allow themselves to changed like that, Billie wondered. Maybe they had their reasons. Maybe they had no choice; maybe it was all a big mistake; maybe they didn't like being human; maybe they didn't want to suffer anymore.

The Machines gave no indication of recognizing individuals. Billie remembered in years past, watching the helter-skelter of the Machine as it slowly expanded into the desert. There were buildings and trees that did not persist. And people, whole crowds of people that winked into and out of existence as quickly as a thought. It was daunting. One image flashing after another, like a million history holos all jumbled up and running in fast forward. Do they grow in any meaningful way, Billie wondered.

Finian would ask what modes of growth are meaningful and want to deconstruct the concept, while Hannah would wonder about their well-being. But what Billie wanted to know is, what do they experience? What is it like to be part of a Machine City which encompassed millions of people for hundreds of years?

Billie was lost in the gulf between. She simply did not know; she could not know. She could look at external signs; she could wonder and project, but she could never experience just what the Machine City folk felt and thought. It made her deeply curious; and it terrified her. The distance between minds, loomed like the distance between stars. Inevitably she left the Machines disturbed — shaken to the core, fragile and appreciative of the natural world, the solid world, her simple self. One time she ran, wildly and heedlessly into the desert. Another time she had collapsed in inconsolable grief.

Again and again, Billie found herself wondering — what human modality were the Machines extending? The whole person? The city? The world? Maybe when the paradigm broke down, the Machine was a person? Maybe this outcome was implicit once homo sapiens started down the tool-maker path? Slowly, as she searched, Billie climbed out of her wonderment, out of herself. By late afternoon she had determined there were no more bugs in the vicinity, and set out for the next water hole.

The next day found Billie in familiar territory. She paused to do a scan of the countryside, climbing a small outcropping of Precambrian rock. In the midmorning sun, the rock was already getting too warm to touch comfortably for long. Ahead she could see the large plasteel pyramid near the entrance to the artificial caves where the disembodied voice lived.

One night, on her very first run alone, she had slept, unwittingly, nearby. In the middle of the night, she had been awakened by music and, perhaps foolishly, had followed the sound down into the caves. It was old miltech and that made her afraid, but she was curious and the music was delightful. At length her torch had guttered and she had been about to turn back, when soft lights had come on along the hallway floor. She had come to a door which would not open, but that was also where the music issued forth. Billie had spent a strange and disjointed night listening to music and trying to talk to the voice. It could hear her, but did not seem to be able to learn. Most of what it said made no sense. It talked about the planetary grid, power allotments, cryonic temperatures, all in some kind of officialese jumble. It didn't know about the wars or the way the world was now. A strangely elated and confused Billie had stumbled out of the caves into bright sunlight and promptly slept half the day away.

Now she moved closer to the pyramid, cautiously pausing to look around again. She had narrowly avoided running into Ultras here once and she did not want to repeat that experience. After watching and listening for a spell, she approached the underground entrance. Inside, the hallway lights did not turn on as they usually did. Billie made her way in the dark by memory. At the end of the hall, the voice was silent. Billie pushed buttons and talked, but nothing happened. A chastened and sad young woman returned to the sunlight. Wiping tunnel grime from her hands, she wondered what elegy was appropriate for an artificial intelligence that never knew it was alive. You are gone with your makers now musician. Play for them as you did for me. It was many kilometres before she shook the feeling.

◆

The temperature was falling fast with the setting sun when Billie glimpsed the Last Bush. She was tired and thirsty, still she maintained her discipline. Closer, she crouched beside some large boulders and scanned along the line of stunted trees and scraggly bushes. The old riverbed was only wet in early spring. It was a wonder anything grew at all.

In one place, she saw sparrows flittering, and when the wind caught the sound, she heard them too. It was a good sign. With a rising enthusiasm, Billie finished her scan. It did not take her long to cover the final two kilometres to the trees and by that time it was dark. She quickly replenished her water and started a fire. Tomorrow she would see what there was to hunt; tonight she was glad just to rest by open water.

Billie slept later than usual. Perhaps it was the shade afforded by the gully and bushes, perhaps she felt more secure for not being exposed. At any rate when she finally did arise, she was chagrined to discover the sun already up. Over her head sparrows twittered. She watched the small creatures bob and whirl as she munched a simple breakfast. The strange bird she had heard the week before tickled the back of her mind.

As was her plan, Billie followed the Last Bush creek westward. Walking beside the thin trickle of water lolling down one side of what had once been a much wider river, she moved much more slowly than on open ground, studying the plants and birds. The only birds were the sparrows, as far as she saw, but there were willow, the odd poplar and at least two different grasses. She did not see the rats, but she heard the whistles, saw the holes in the bank and knew they were about, which was good because her dried dog meat was almost gone. During the spring surge of plant life near the water, an annoying type of small midge propagated explosively. It was one of the few insect life forms remaining and seemed sometimes to have the sole purpose of getting in her eyes. Billie followed the Last Bush closer to the Dead City watching for trailsign. By noon, she was ten kilometres to the west travelling slowly, but steadily, along the creek. In a couple of months she would have to dig for water here.

The distant distinctive drone on an Ultra aircar became audible. Billie scrambled across the old riverbed to the far bank and crawled up to the edge. She found the car in her vuscope and followed it. The vehicle swung around to the southeast and stopped about a kilometre back along the creek. It rose again, turned in a circle and then began approaching slowly.

Billie cast about for a means of escape. She could not run. The land was flat on either side. She had to hide. She darted across the riverbed and slid down behind a thick clump of bushes.

The aircar came around the bend and floated right up the riverbed to settle across from her position. The vehicle was vaguely brick-shaped with rounded corners. A single window wrapped around the front of the vehicle. The motor stopped. The Ultra who emerged was blue, with four arms. He was tall like all of the Ultras, about two and a quarter metres high, and completely hairless. He wore loose, three-quarter length pants and an open-sided sort of poncho top which accommodated his arms. In one pair of hands, the Ultra held a long-barrelled weapon. In another hand, he held a scanning device. He looked like a pretty boy or a masculine girl, with smooth regular features. The Ultra did not look up, but spun in a slow circle watching the device in his hand with a frown.

"Come out, little human, I know you are there." The Ultra spoke in a soft, high-pitched lilt. He stopped turning, looking right at Billie's clump of willows. "Ah, there you are. Come out, little one. I have a gift for you."

Billie stood trembling and wondering what the Ultra was doing. The creature smiled with a peculiar expression, part disdain, part sardonic patrimony. He beckoned with his free arm.

"You will like this. Come and see." The Ultra turned and walked toward the back of the aircar. Billie stood frozen. The Ultra stopped and commanded, "Well, come on. I don't have all day."

With a jolt Billie started to follow. She came around the back of the craft to see the Ultra standing beside a heavy metallic ramp, his face still locked in that peculiar grin. He seemed to be greatly amused by something. He was acting like the master of ceremonies of his own little three ring circus. The Ultra touched something on his belt and a big freight door opened in the back of the aircar. He waved her forward again. Inside the aircar were four terrified and bedraggled looking young buffalo.

"These are a gift to you humans, and the world," He proclaimed magnanimously. The Ultra paused and then it was like a switch had been thrown. He changed moods and direction on the head of a pin. "Now get them out of the truck. My time is short." He gestured sharply.

Billie climbed into the back and moved slowly along one side of the compartment toward the front. The buffalo were nervous and tried to edge away from her. When Billie reached the front, the animals suddenly decided to bolt out the back. With a clatter of hooves and a snort they were outside and away.

The Ultra laughed in a high-pitched voice as Billie jumped down. The buffalo were twenty metres away and still running. "See that wasn't so bad," he added in a frozen-faced, patronizing tone.

"You can't just leave them here," said Billie. "They will never survive. In another month this water will be gone and the grass all dead."

The Ultra turned and examined Billie with arch disdain. "They will live or they will die according to their attributes and circumstance. There are others further north, but it may be these," he gestured to the buffalo with his free hand, "who are furthest from humans, who thrive."

To this blunt assessment, Billie had nothing to say. She watched silently as the Ultra closed the back of the car. While Billie thought about the buffalo, the Ultra climbed into the front. In a moment the aircar was rising and pulling away. Billie stood and watched it shrink to a dot and disappear.

The buffalo were out of sight to the east. She shook her head and resumed her slow trek westward along the creek bed. Her thoughts whirled. She felt diminished somehow. She didn't understand it or like it. Billie tried to direct her thoughts toward the future. In another week, she would break south toward the Dead City. What other species have the Ultras introduced, she wondered. And why were they doing that? While she wrestled with her discomfort, it occurred to her the Ultra had not even considered taking her back north. Why not? They were so unpredictable. Billie tried to focus her thoughts on the here and now, but they kept slipping away in wonder and dread.

The Dead City

Abstract:

The biotic crisis overtaking our planet is likely to precipitate a major extinction of species. That much is well known. Not so well known but probably more significant in the long term is that the crisis will surely disrupt and deplete certain basic processes of evolution, with consequences likely to persist for millions of years. Distinctive features of future evolution could include a homogenization of biotas, a proliferation of opportunistic species, a pest-and-weed ecology, an outburst of speciation among taxa that prosper in human-dominated ecosystems, a decline of biodisparity, an end to the speciation of large vertebrates, the depletion of "evolutionary powerhouses" in the tropics, and unpredictable emergent novelties. Despite this likelihood, we have only a rudimentary understanding of how we are altering the evolutionary future. As a result of our ignorance, conservation policies fail to reflect long-term evolutionary aspects of biodiversity loss.

— Norman Myers and Andrew H. Knoll[1]

✦

---

[1] "The biotic crisis and the future of evolution"
by Norman Myers and Andrew H. Knoll
PNAS 2001 98: 5389-5392.
Copyright (2001) National Academy of Sciences, U.S.A.
URL: http://www.pnas.org/cgi/content/abstract/98/10/5389

DAY IN DAY OUT, THE WIND blew steadily from the southwest. Many global weather patterns had changed with the dramatic rise in temperature, the loss of trees and the reshaped land, but not the sou'westers. The prevailing winds prevailed. Billie tended to move early in the day, stop in mid-afternoon, set snares and then investigate nearby landmarks of interest — buildings, towers, old wrecks, all the while watching out for bugs and Ultras. She had food; she had water; she had time — and the wind, always the wind. A fine grit coated everything. Any object left in the open grew drifts of sandy dust, miniature dunes which rode the backs of larger dunes — simplicity piled upon simplicity yielding complexity.

For three weeks Billie worked her way along the Last Bush. She did not see another soul. The night before she came to the notched tree which marked the point to turn south towards the Dead City, a violent electrical storm raged far ahead in that direction. Billie sat in a tree and watched the sheet lightning, the ground strikes far away. Low black clouds hugged the horizon. Only the odd rumble of distant thunder was audible, but still it was a magnificent and panoramic display.

The next morning, there was not a cloud in the sky. Billie came to the notched tree, filled her water bottles and struck out southward. It was four days to the Dead City and there was only one well on this stretch. In late afternoon while looking for shelter, she came across a curious sight. In a slight valley which had evidently been visited by the storm the night before, water had collected and dissolved some mineral in the soil. The water was gone, but it had left a pattern of crystals as it evaporated, large in the centre and progressively smaller toward the edge. The remarkable sight rang a chord in the back of Billie's mind. For a moment she was dazzled — lost in the wonder of molecule and crystal. Her thirst soon reminded her to move.

Late in the third day she glimpsed the skyline of the Dead City floating like a mirage. The towers were so tall and they were visible from so far away, that it seemed to Billie she walked forever and never got any closer. Come sundown, Billie took shelter in an empty warehouse on the outskirts. There was no point in pushing for the tower she decided; she wouldn't be able to see at night anyway.

The next morning Billie walked up an old concrete highway leading into the city centre. She had a love-hate relationship with the ghost city. There were so many places an enemy could hide. So many little nooks and crannies. And yet, at the same time, it was exotic and awe inspiring, magnificent and humbling. From time to time, she disturbed skeletons or bones, but one got used to that. They had been dead for so long. It was not at all sepulchral. As she followed the road up across a freeway bridge, Billie felt briefly like she was riding an ancient dinosaur. The Old Ones and she were insects riding a great clanking beast to the horizon.

The concrete road lead through what had been a residential district. Billie walked one side of the flat hard surface watching the nearby sand for tracks. Most of the nearby buildings which had been made of wood were crumbling. A flash of light reflected from a piece of old window or solar panel. The houses went on for kilometre after kilometre, depressingly all the same. One peculiar thing about the city was it could all begin to seem so normal. As she neared the downtown section with the largely undamaged plasteel buildings, she could almost imagine one of the Old Ones walking around a corner, but nothing moved on the streets not even tumbleweed. There were no signs of life. Even the rats have gone she thought.

One of the downtown skyscrapers had collapsed since last year. Debris filled the street and she had to detour. In the medium distance stood her goal, the tallest of the old city towers. From the top of that building, Billie knew, she could see a circle many kilometres wide. It was three hundred sixteen levels; six hundred thirty four flights of stairs with one detour to the other end of the building where something had smashed into the side of the tower and gouged out a hunk four floors deep. She knew because once in exhausted determination she had counted them.

Gradually she made her way towards the tall tower. The desert was claiming the city. It was being scoured clean by the perpetual winds. Nothing grew. Every once in a while she stopped to look for bugs with her vuscope. High overhead a fleck in motion caught Billie's eye. For a moment she watched it soar. The wings did not move and it was silent. She thought of the bird she had heard that night a month before, and quickly fished her vuscope out of her shoulder bag, but by the time she looked up again, the bird was gone. She continued toward the tower, dividing her time between the sky and the ground, but saw no further sign of the bird. Billie was glad to get inside, out of the wind, and out of sight, even if it did mean a severe climb. She took her time, rested every fifty floors and had a drink of water and a longer rest every hundred. It only seemed to take forever, she told herself when she reached the top of the stairwell.

A utility ladder built into the wall led up to a hatch whose lock she had jimmied years before. On the roof, it was windy as usual. Billie stood in the middle of the roof in the shade of a block structure with no doors or windows, letting her heart slow down. She gazed at the countryside around the tower. Heat waves made the horizon shimmer and dance. Beside her on the deck was a patch of bird lime. Billie carefully stepped on it and twisted to mark it. The outside wall of the tower projected up to mid-chest and it made a convenient, if warm, ledge on which to lean. She walked around the perimeter, stopping at the odd place, making a quick survey. The nuclear blast to the south was perfectly smooth. The rest of the horizon seemed unchanged as well. She saw no bugs in her casual inspection. Later she would take more time to look more carefully.

Billie decided to make camp. On a previous trip she had spent hours removing every thing from one of the rooms on the floor below. Her own behaviour had puzzled her a little, as she had dragged all the tables, couches, desks and equipment from one room, but she went with it. Then sitting in the empty room, with her back to a wall, she had decided she wanted a chair after all, and then she needed a table, and the tile on plasteel floor was too hard. She had never done anything about the floor beyond a blanket, but she had found a small steel folding chair and a simple wood and plastic box for a table and the room, somehow, was hers.

Her room was undisturbed. Billie dropped her things just inside the door and went to take a quick look around. The interior halls were roughly 'H' shaped, with her room near one foot of the 'H', just down the hall from the ladder to the roof. At the other side and end of the building, behind hallway dividing doors, some glass panels were missing. Sand had drifted in that side and end of the hallway. There were no tracks, no sign of life.

Back in her room Billie settled in. She unpacked her shoulder bag on the box table and, taking only her vuscope and knives, went back up on roof. She spent the rest of the day, peering through her vuscope, examining the city and countryside. For the bugs, the city was a huge store of refined materials and if they became entrenched, they would be hard to extirpate. Slowly, section by section she scanned the surrounding districts.

When the sun got low in the west, and it became difficult to see well, Billie went back downstairs to eat. She examined her supplies. She had water for another week, which was enough to take a good look around here and make it back to the Last Bush with no problem. Food was not a problem. She still had a bit of dog meat and she had found lots of rat along the creek. She took out the last bit of Stirling biscuit she had been saving as a treat.

As she enjoyed her feast, she heard a thump in the exterior hallway. Billie froze. Silently she rose, picked up her knife and edged into the adjoining room, filled with old furniture and the remains of arcane equipment after the wood and plastic had been eaten away. Billie slipped through the room. She peeked one way, and then the other at the hallway door. There was nothing in sight. Slowly she once again made her way around the floor. She saw no sign of another, nothing untoward. She was puzzled. She did not see that anything had fallen either. Perhaps it was the wind, or the building settling she decided uneasily. She was still quite on her guard as she moved slowly through the darkening building, back toward her room.

A thin white boy sat in her steel chair, grinning at her like an idiot.

"Who the hell are you?" she demanded. "And what are you doing here?" she added for good measure.

The boy just kept grinning. He smiled and pointed to the southwest. "I came up from the south looking for . . . "

"Out of the badlands?!" Billie interrupted.

The boy nodded.

"Impossible!" snorted Billie. "Nothing lives there. You'd never survive."

"I did," the boy stated simply.

Billie stared at him. He was thin, very thin; skeletal and young — a teenager. His bone white, angular face was triangular — wide at the temples and narrow at the chin. What hair he had was short, very short; His arms appeared to be hairless. His skin looked more like plastic than flesh. It reminded Billy of a patch of factory skin one of the old villagers sported. But who was he and had he really come out of the badlands? It didn't seem likely. She crossed the room to the window, putting what little light there was at her back.

In fact, Billie had only forayed short distances south of the city into the badlands and even that had been formidable. She had never found good water to the south and her mentor, Jack, had not known of any either. She thought of the wasteland the North American continent had become, ringed by the wild Machines. The nano devices had taken the far south and the coasts, anywhere there was warmth. They had never gone north of the desert because of the cold. The Yellowstone mantle plume had reopened and put finished to the desertification that global warming had started. South of the city, nothing remained but sand and ruins. Unless he was from the Water Lodge.

"What tribe are you?" demanded Billie.

"What do you mean? I have no tribe." The kid looked at blankly. "Are you some kind of Indian or something?"

Billie smiled at the archaism. He does not know the People she thought. He is not from the Water Lodge. Which meant he was either telling the truth or it was some kind of elaborate trick, maybe an Ultra trick. She didn't put anything past them.

"What's your name anyway?" she asked in a more conversational tone. The boy continued with his idiotic grin. He seemed to have only the one mode.

"Can't rightly say as I have one," the boy replied in a peculiarly slow and measured way. Almost as though he were some Southern gentleman. Or what? wondered Billie. He didn't look right at Billie very often; almost never made eye contact.

"My parents never did name me. They just called me Kid." A flicker of dread danced over his face and disappeared. "Then the army came and took me. They called me Harmer, but I don't like that name."

Billie smiled ingenuously and nodded. She did not believe a word the boy said. There had not been an army, anywhere, for hundreds of years. She shifted gears into a gathering information with honey mode without skipping a beat. She chuckled. "That's like me. My name is Wilhemina, but I go by Billie, because I hate the way it sounds."

The boy smiled. It was the first real emotion Billie had seen him show. It was soon gone, replaced by the idiotic grin.

"So what shall I call you? I can't just say 'hey you' all the time," Billie prompted.

The boy looked thoughtful for a moment. "Kid will do. Just call me Kid."

Billie was not quite sure what to make of this declaration, but she took it at face value. "Okay Kid, now why are you coming north?" She did her best to sound as if they were old friends.

"I am looking for people." the Kid replied. "It's a big empty land and you're the first person I have seen since . . . " He fell silent. Billie waited. The Kid appeared to wage some silent, interior war. He caught himself and finished. " . . . and then I saw you coming."

"Oh. Have you been here long?"

"A couple of days."

"You pick out your own place?"

"What do you mean?"

"Where did you sleep? I didn't see any sign. Do you have your own room?"

"No. I just sleep wherever I happen to be."

"Okay. Well if you don't mind I would like to be alone now. I need to sleep."

"Uh sure. Okay." The Kid stood up and came over beside Billie at the window. He moved with scarcely a sound.

Peering at her intently in the dim light he said, "You've been asking a lot of questions, but what are you doing here? I did not expect to find anyone in this desolation."

Billie was not sure just how much she wished to tell this stranger. She opted for a name, instead of an explanation. "I'm a Ranger."

"A Ranger? What does that mean?"

"I patrol the frontier."

"The frontier of what?"

"The People's territory."

"The People!" The kids eyes went wide and he repeated the word like a talisman. "The People. There are more people?"

Billie nodded.

"I've been looking for people, and there is nobody . . . " he nodded to the south.

Billie could see him more clearly now that he stood in the light and the nearness made her uneasy. She felt viscerally that the Kid was dangerous, even though he was so slight. She did not know, did not trust him.

"I can take you to the lodge, but I have to finish my run first. Or you can go that way yourself," she pointed west northwest away from the lodge, and in a sudden air of apparent bonhomie, added, "If you go about fifteen hundred kilometres in that direction, you'll run into them." She paused for a second. "And if you miss them, you'll run into the Arctic Ocean and then if you follow the coastline west, you'll run into the Water Lodge." She was going to know this stranger a lot better before she considered taking him anywhere near the Lodge.

"People. There are people," the Kid repeated in a lingering daze.

"Yes. Now if you don't mind . . . " Billie took him by the arm and started moving him toward the door. The white, white skin felt strangely cold. "I need to sleep."

"Oh yes. Of course," said the Kid, as though catching himself out and suddenly remembering his manners. At the door he stopped, and a touch of the southern gentleman reappeared. "Good night, ma'am," he said, and quickly disappeared into the dark.

As Billie fell asleep, the strange feeling of the Kid's arm lingered in the back of her mind like a taste of metal that would not go away. It occurred to her that not once in their time together had he checked out her body. Usually every man did it without thinking, but he had never looked at her sexually. He had hardly looked right at her at all. His eyes had watched her hands, her midriff, but it felt different, cooler somehow. Mostly he had looked around her. It made her vaguely uneasy. The funny cold plastic feeling of his arm tickled the back of her mind throughout the night.

The next morning before dawn, Billie stashed her shoulder bag out of sight and headed for the roof with her vuscope and a water bottle. She did a quick once around again, and then resumed her methodical scan of the city and surrounding land. The ring on the outskirts directly to the south, where the nuclear device had flattened and fused a circle kilometres wide, was the easiest to inspect in the dim light, so she started there. She could not see it all, but what was in view, was flat and featureless. The district was motionless. In midmorning the Kid came up beside her and watched for a while.

"What are you doing?" he asked.

"Looking for bugs — wild nano," she replied without taking her eyes from the vuscope.

"Yeah? What are you going to with them if you do find them?" the Kid scoffed.

Billie turned and looked at him. She noticed with some surprise that the Kid was turning decidedly darker, almost black. "Kill them," she said with a quiet intensity.

"Now that would be a good trick."

Billie continued her scanning and some time later she noticed the Kid had disappeared. He sure can move quietly that one she thought to herself. A while later she made a quick trip downstairs for her hat and a bite to eat. The Kid was not downstairs either.

The weather stayed remarkably calm and it got quite hot on the roof. By late afternoon Billie was relatively sure there were no bugs within ten or twelve kilometres of the tower, which was about as far as she could reliably examine. As she headed downstairs, she realized she had decided, somehow without thinking about it, to take the Kid with her on the rest of her run. It seemed to be the sensible thing to do. She would learn more about him as they travelled together and the lingering danger she felt in him would not be shared by any other. Billie paused at the top of the ladder. The Kid was soaking up the sun lying flat on his back on the top of the block over the elevator shaft. He was coal black and naked. An involuntary quickening moved in her and her breath hitched. The image of his nakedness played across her mind, as she climbed down the ladder. She had to know more about this stranger. Perhaps a little sexy sugar to draw the fly, she mused. Billie dismissed the thought, but the image of his jet black, ultra smooth skin would not go away.

She ate her simple supper and tried not to think of the Kid by focusing on the trail ahead. When later he came downstairs, the

Kid walked right by Billie's room without speaking. She looked up to catch a glimpse of white skin flashing past the darkening doorway. He had changed colour again. An image of the great lodge full of children all changing colour, black, white, black, white flashed through Billie's mind. She chuckled and the hard thought struck, but not with me. It was many hours before she slept that night.

The day broke cold and hard under a cloudless sky. The sun was just peeking over the horizon as Billie took a quick and final look around the roof. Again nothing moved. The Kid was not around. Billie chewed on old bannock sipping a little water. She was not worried about keeping track of the Kid. He wanted people. He would show up sooner or later. She steeled herself to tackle the stairs, packed her few things and clomped down the stairs purposefully making noise. Back down on the street, Billie was not more than fifty metres from the skyscraper before the Kid emerged through a broken ground floor window.

"Hey wait for me." he called.

Billie turned back momentarily, and then continued only a little more slowly. When the Kid caught up to her she turned and spoke forcefully. "You keep up. We go when I say we go and we go where I say we go. This is my country and I know it. If you are not careful, it will kill you."

The Kid was unfazed. "Okay but wait a sec." He dropped his old miltech backpack on the ground and started fishing inside. He pulled out a heads-up display that fit over the top of his head and curved behind his ear. A short metal rod with what looked like a piece of glass projected in front of his right eye. He fumbled with some control just over his ear, then apparently satisfied, resumed rummaging through the backpack and pulled out a grey-coloured ball about ten centimetres in diameter. He looked at the sun once quickly, and then held the ball in front of himself, squeezed it purposefully and threw it into the air.

Billie stepped back startled. The ball unfolded and transformed itself into a small airplane. The nanocarbon exterior stiffened, caught the breeze and lifted. It was the stiff bird she had seen flying overhead two days before.

"I usually avoid using radio here, because it tends to draw Ultras," said Billie.

"Who?" asked the Kid.

Billie just looked at him for a second, thinking how best to explain. "They were created by the Old Ones; they're all different colours and some have four or six arms."

"Oh them. Is that what you call them? Ultras. Well, to answer your worry, it's optical internally and it uses highly directional point-to-point ultraviolet for communication," replied the Kid, adjusting the display." The only way the Ultras might detect it was if they were in low-earth orbit."

"And what makes you think they are not?" Billie rejoindered and was satisfied to see the self-assured look disappear from his face. At least, she thought, I know he has run into Ultras before.

"No matter, then," she decided aloud. "We'll take the chance and use it. I rather like the idea of being able to see from above. I'll have to get Finian to crank me one of these."

The kid looked at her like she was talking bafflegab, and she did not explain. They walked toward the southwest, away from the sun, their shadows long in front of them. Billie noticed, now that they were together continuously, how the Kid gradually darkened as the sun brightened. By mid-morning he was coal black.

On the edge of town, the Kid pointed to an old concrete road running along a slight ridge ahead and said, "This is where I came into town. You'll see my tracks over there."

Billie picked up the trail, and they headed south following the same path. The Kid looked at Billie oddly from time to time, as if wondering why they were following his tracks, but he said nothing.

At some point during the morning, the Kid had picked up a walking stick, which he used to test ground and to point. Billie did not see where it had come from.

It was a distinctly different feeling for Billie to be not alone in the southern wastes. She found herself being startled from time to time when the Kid wandered off and reappeared. He used the drone whenever they were moving, which looked a little strange. Billie could see peripheral light refracting from the heads-up display or reflecting from his eye, whenever she looked at him.

She had only the water she carried. Billie had surveyed this area for wells years before, so she knew what to expect. They travelled late, made camp in the lee of an old stone wall and slept soundly. Towards the end of the next day, the Kid's trail was almost gone. The steady wind had drifted sand and dust across the open areas and she was only picking up a mark here and there. Billie decided there was no point in tracing it further. They swung back toward the northwest.

The Kid came over beside her and said, "So now do you believe I really came out of the badlands?"

Billie looked at him and shrugged. "The First Bush is five or six days that way," she pointed ahead, "and water is at least four."

Sometimes it is difficult to notice an absence. So it was that Billie did not notice until the second day that the Kid did not appear to sweat. She began to pay more attention to what he ate and drank. It was miniscule compared to herself. She started offering the Kid water from her own bottles just to see how he would react. He usually declined. By and large, he did not seem to notice the byplay. Billie was becoming more curious about this stranger.

One day a thunderstorm formed directly ahead of them and bore down suddenly ominous and threatening. Large dark streaks could be seen falling from the bottom of the cloud base. The wind picked up and the blowing dust became uncomfortable. Billie had some protection for her eyes from her hat and sun shield, but the Kid had none. He seemed unperturbed. The storm clouds passed directly overhead. No rain landed.

Gradually Billie came to a grudging acceptance of the Kid. He did not do anything stupid. He spoke only when he had something to say. He was no trouble. He treated her like one of the guys and when she accepted that, she stopped thinking of his touch.

It was a full moon again the night they reached the well. They made camp behind a rusted metal shed. Pieces of old farm equipment littered the ground. Half-covered skeletons poked through the sand. What had been the house had mostly burnt down, but there was wood enough for a fire.

The Kid and Billie collapsed one on either side of the fire. With the deep purple and gold of the western sky and the moon holding water in the east, Billie chewed her half-dry rat. The Kid was eating light again she noted. The fire died down to a bank of embers. There was no wind. The land hung quiet, strangely damp in the evening coolness.

Billie got up to get some more wood. Far, far away in the west, a fluting animal trumpeting broke forth. She froze. It sounded like a call of distress. In a minute Billie started breathing again. She brought an armful of wood back to the fire. The Kid had changed colour, a pattern of light and dark splotches that whitened as he relaxed.

"What the hell was that?" the Kid whispered.

"I don't know. I've never heard anything like it before."

Together they sat and listened, but the sound did not recur.

"Tomorrow I'll have to go and find out," said Billie. The fire died down and they slept.

The next morning when Billie awoke just before dawn, the Kid was gone. She skipped breakfast and headed quickly in the direction of last night's roar. The Kid's footprints were in front of her.

About six kilometres away, Billie came over a small ridge and found the Kid down on his hands and knees peering into the mouth of a large dead lizard. She felt like she was walking into a dream. Billie walked around the creature in rapt wonder. It was beautiful, with overlapping scales of blue and green glistening in the morning sun. She felt like she was swimming in slow motion. The reptile was whole, undecayed. There was no smell. It had not been dead long.

"It was an herbivore. See the teeth." The Kid tapped the side of the creature's mouth with his walking stick.

Billie said one word. "Ultras."

The Kid looked at her quickly. "You think?"

"How else would it get here? Dinosaurs have been extinct for sixty million years. Hell, the amphibians and reptiles have been gone for five hundred plus."

The Kid looked at her strangely and prodded the carcass with his stick again.

"They may be monitoring it," Billie continued. "Let's get out of here." She turned toward the northwest and strode away. The Kid caught up to her and they walked together along the ridge, the sun warming their backs.

"Why would they do that?" the Kid wondered out loud.

Billie did not answer. She had no answer.

They walked the rest of the morning without seeing or hearing Ultras. Around noon they climbed a rise and saw a large white area stretching toward the west. Sunlight reflected brilliantly from a crystalline surface. Billie led them more northerly, away from its border.

"What is it?" the Kid asked stopping at the top of a small hill to look at it. Billie turned back and decided to take a water break. She sat on the side of the hill facing the whiteness and pulled a water bottle and her vuscope out of her bag. She handed the vuscope to the Kid. He put his eyes to the lens and then pulled away quickly, evidently dazzled by the brightness.

"There is a polarization filter. There, on the side. See." Billie indicated a slightly protruding wheel. The Kid settled down to scanning the whiteness and Billie watched.

"Bad water here, near the big white."

The Kid looked at her. "Yeah, but what is it?"

Billie shrugged. "Something the Old Ones did before the war. There used to be huge tar sands all around here, and someone hit it with a custom petrophilic bacteria which left this alkaline residue. Now the water's bad and the ground looks like that."

Billie took the vuscope back from the Kid and put it in her shoulder bag. "There's another ring like it further north with a poisoned aquifer. And there's even a zone away to the west where there's some drifting nanowire. Have you run into diamond thorns?"

The kid nodded.

"They're a real pain," Billie grumbled. "You have to remove each one separately." She shook her head sagely. "The Old Ones." She started down the hill towards the north.

After a while the Kid came up beside Billie. "There's a tower in the centre."

She stopped and looked at him. "Yes, I know. Sometimes when it is really hot, you can see it in a mirage. How did you . . ." She broke off and finished "Oh the drone." Billie grinned at him. "Well don't lose it in there. You wouldn't like to have to go and get it." She kept going north.

◆

It was a couple of days before Billie saw the Last Bush. When they reached it, she felt like she was home free. It was nice to be sheltered from the constant wind and she had food and water again. They travelled in the old riverbed, beside the little water that still ran. The days fell quickly into a rhythm — travel in the morning, break early, set snares, then poke around and explore a lot.

One afternoon Billie was climbing a tall tree to hang rat meat to dry above the midges, when suddenly it seemed unnaturally quiet. There was . . . a certain stillness. She turned to examine the western sky.

"Oh shit!" she exclaimed, "Its too early in the year!" She shinnied down the tree in a hurry.

"What's the matter?" asked the Kid.

"Sandstorm." Billie pointed to the west where a black cloud could now be seen advancing across the country.

"Oh." He replied as though he wondered what all the fuss was about. "It looks like it is mostly going to miss us."

Billie turned and looked at him like he was an idiot. "No. It won't miss us. It's heading south east, but it is wide. Look." She pointed to the swirling edge of the black cloud that even now was billowing in their direction. "We have to make shelter. Fast."

She ran down the gully. The Kid looked after her apparently puzzled.

Billie stopped by a clump of grey willow. "This will do just fine." In ten minutes she had cut the centre out using her knife, leaving just enough room for herself and the Kid. She wound branches from either side together, notching some over the top to catch each other and make a small dome shaped structure. The ones she had cut out of the centre she wove into the walls. By now the wind was beginning to gust erratically kicking up small stones. She went back down the gully and retrieved her shoulder bag. She pushed it through the low entrance to the dome and turned to the Kid. "Come on get inside."

He was putting on a strange looking jacket he had pulled from his pack. Once the Kid had it on, it seemed to inflate. He pulled a hood up and smoothed some velcro straps in place. A filter piece covered his mouth and nose, and a section of clear plastic that would function as goggles.

"No. You go ahead. I'll be alright," the Kid yelled back over the rising wind.

With no time to argue, Billie scuttled off down the creek cutting more branches for her shelter. She dragged an armful back and wove them into the wall of her shelter. The Kid started helping her. The wind was blasting now and they could not talk, but only shout.

"What is it?" Billie yelled in his ear, pinching the inflated jacket. She could feel slippery layers of material moving inside under her fingers.

"A desert suit." the Kid shouted back. "You had better go inside."

Stubbornly, with her eyes open only a crack, Billie finished weaving the last of her branches into the dome. She crawled through the low entrance. Inside the wind was reduced but still palpable. The dust was everywhere. She wrapped her head in her poncho and collapsed. Billie lay curled up listening to the shrieking winds. She would have to ask the Kid about sandstorms in the south, and maybe take a good look at that desert suit. Suddenly she had nothing to do. The forced immobility sneaked up on her and she fell sound asleep. The storm raged the rest of the day and died sometime during the night.

Billie awoke before dawn feeling like an idiot. What a stupid thing to do, she upbraided herself. The low entrance was half-full of sand and her shoulder bag was buried. A momentary fear crossed her mind as she imagined being buried by the sand while asleep. She let her fear go and set about unweaving her little dome to make another exit.

Outside, she heard the Kid clear his throat. He was sitting still with his back against the shelter wall beside the entrance, like he had not moved. The day was still and crystal clear, one of those magical mornings. The sun was just hinting in the east.

The Kid watched with some amusement as Billie disassembled her wind shelter.

"Why bother?" he asked just as she finished.

"What I cut can be used as firewood sometime. The rest will grow better if it is not twisted in an unnatural shape."

"If its not buried by the next storm," the Kid said.

"The land is all," said Billie simply. "What I preserve today, may preserve me tomorrow. I leave no footprint." She took her bag and headed west. It would be three weeks before they got to the Big Tree and there was no point in standing around. She wondered vaguely where the drying rat meat had ended up as she passed the tattered remnants of the tree she had been climbing.

The Mission

And death shall have no dominion — Dylan Thomas

◆

Project	*Human contact*
Task	*Homo sapiens contact*
Identity	*TFM-7356-1926-4366*
Timestamp	*0x0000:000B:B443:2CA8*
Location	*235, 543, 789*
Energy Status	*Nominal, external supplies available*
Comm Status:	*Nominal*
System Status:	*Nominal*
Human Status:	*Nominal*
Human Comment:	*Search for homo sapiens continuing.*

Intercepted satellite data has revealed two specimens near this location.

◆

PROGRESS DOWN THE OLD RIVERBED WAS slow because some sections were piled high with sand. Several times the Kid and Billie had to make little excursions out of the riverbed itself. Billie wondered what the runoff waters from the Arctic rains would do next year. Build up and cut through, she guessed. Oddly enough, some sections of the riverbed were practically untouched. In a couple of days, they cleared the district the storm had touched and the easy rhythm of morning travel and afternoon hunting resumed.

"We should be coming up on the Big Tree soon," said Billie one afternoon and the next day they could see it gleaming silver in the distance. The Big Tree was a dead deciduous genmod. The wind had stripped the bark and smaller branches leaving a stark silver giant towering over the scrub willow and poplar along the creek. In daytime the tree loomed large and impressive; at night it was more so. It glowed with an eerie and spectral half-light due to the inserted genes for bioluminescence. The biowarriors liked to leave such distinctive little signatures in their handiwork.

Now the tree stood tall and true, a silver sentinel reminding those who would hear what life had once been along this waterway. To Billie it was a landmark, a turning point. A little further to the west, the old riverbed turned south and she would swing northwest, travelling again from well to well across the open country. By midday they had reached the tree.

"We'll make camp over there," Billie pointed to a smaller tree just to the west.

"What's the matter with here?" asked the Kid.

"Nothing. It's less obtrusive there, is all. Travellers always come to the Big Tree first."

It was clear that the spot by the smaller tree had been used before. A ring of rocks circled the remains of older fires. Billie dropped her bag on the bank and started climbing the small tree to look around.

The flier was silent — a floating squished flat teardrop shape. Billie did not notice it, and neither did the Kid, until the explosion. She was sitting on a branch watching the Kid compact his flying drone when it happened. The aircar had come over a slight ridge just to the southwest. Now it slid forward tilting at an angle, with smoke pouring from a hole in the back right surface. Billie froze. The aircar careened toward them. The Kid had disappeared. A white vapour trailed from the vehicle, which rose as though attempting to leap the gully and then abruptly crunched nose down in the sand and muck of the riverbed.

Everything seemed to stop. Sitting in the tree, Billie watched with fascination and some small alarm as a side panel opened and out stumbled a large silver manshape. He staggered towards Billie, holding his hand out beseechingly. "Hello," she called. The stranger's mouth was moving, but no sound emerged. "Are you okay?" The Kid arose from behind the bushes with a crossbow in his hands. Now where did he get that, Billie wondered. His skin had become black and white and green in that miltech camouflage pattern again. The stranger raised his hand and the Kid let fly with a bolt.

To Billie's amazement, the stranger instantaneously grew a layer of body armour across his torso, reaching from neck to crotch. The bolt bounced. The stranger's mouth was still working silently. The Kid was busy fitting another bolt and it all struck Billie as absurd. She started to laugh. The silver stranger took another weak step and pitched face forward into the muck of the creek.

✦

Project:	*<data corruption>*
Task:	*<data corruption>*
Identity:	TFM-7356-1926-4366
Timestamp	0x0000:000B:B443:48C3
Location	246, 554, 790
Energy Status:	Low, external supplies damaged
Comm Status:	Errored out

System Status:	*Multiple, concomitant failures*
Human Status:	*Unknown*

Human Comment: *There is a long black tunnel stretching out to light, out to the world. And where does it arise? What is this enveloping darkness? What is this slow motion swimming through the amniotic —- this swamp teeming with life, with possibility, with tomorrows? The machine is damaged. I am damaged. I open my eyes. There are no clouds. A blue green sky. The sound of water running. My implant is dead. I cannot hear the One, the Many. That should never happen. I am scared. Have I been unconscious? For how long? What has happened? I luxuriate in golden sunlight pouring down like liquid honey, and then I see her sitting in the crook of an old willow, watching me. I cannot contact her. I should be able to contact her at this distance. She is damaged or I am damaged. She moves very slowly, sitting in the tree swinging a leg. She starts moving her mouth, making noises. She is talking! She is a primitive! The sounds have meaning. These are words, language, speech. I have to remember the old way again. I cannot hear the One, the Many. She is laughing.*

✦

"What do you think you are going to do to him?" laughed Billie scornfully.

The Kid spun around with a wild-eyed desperate look on his face. "We should kill him now," he shouted.

"No. I've never seen anything like that aircar before. We should find out who he is at least. We don't even know where he's from."

The Kid was getting agitated. "He had something in his hand." He was breathing quickly looking back and forth between her and the silver stranger. "We must remove the immediate danger." The Kid sounded ritualistic, like he was reciting a military manual.

"Look. He's injured. We can deal with him. Calm down."

"No!" the Kid screamed. "I won't endanger my life for your curiosity." He spun around and shot at Billie. The dart struck her in the chest and she fell backwards from the tree. She hit the ground headfirst and did not move. The Kid went over to her, his face a tautly drawn mask. It looked like her neck was broken and the bolt had taken her heart. He stalked the fallen stranger. When he got closer, he could see it was an artificial life form. A flap of grey metallic skull had broken open above the right ear. On the side of the neck, the letters TFM and some numbers were visible. It was partly covered by the body armour.

Suddenly he was confused. There was no danger. There. Was. Nothing. Wrong. It had happened again! He had killed needlessly, automatically. It was like the battle. The army. He spun in a welter of old memories. The killing didn't stop until there was nobody left to kill. The frenzy! The carnage! The sounds of the wounded and dying. Explosions! Instant death, from above, from below, from inside. And when the sound died down and the killing stopped, there were no emotions. There was no thought. The programming erased the person. There was no one to be. No one. For a time, the Kid did not have a recognizable thought. An extraordinary inner silence flowed over him. He saw; the world was; he reacted. There was nothing else. He staggered dazedly away behind the burning aircar, blindly trying to escape his pain and confusion.

Externally, the end of the bolt protruding from Billie's chest fell off. The wound appeared to seal and heal in fast forward. Her head moved and her neck straightened out. She appeared to become ten years younger. Her skin became slightly darker. She started to breath. She moaned and put a hand to her head.

Internally, Restart nano assemblers in Billie's skeletal structure recognized that she had died. Her heart, lung and brain activity had stopped. Powered by tapping the quantum flux, the tiny machines began to multiply and migrate. Atom by atom, the nanobots rebuilt her body to a precise duplicate of the twenty-year-old girl who had first taken the Restart imprint in the great lodge years before. The body, but not the brain. In this instance, the brain was largely undamaged and so left untouched. Arteries, veins, skull, glial cells and other support structures were rebuilt; the neurons and the myriad dendritic connections were unchanged.

Billie woke up on the ground with a headache feeling like she wanted to puke. It was always this way. The replicated nano assemblers congregated in the upper stomach and turned themselves off when they had finished their job. It was Billie's seventh death and she recognized the Restart phenomena when she awoke. She remembered how frenzied the Kid had become — and the stranger. Harmer, had shot her. She could no longer think of the black white colour changing teenager as the Kid. He was now Harmer. Her next thought was that there was no one to do the ritual. She threw up once, violently, and sat. She started the Ritual When Alone. "I recognize these hands. I recognize these feet. I recognize . . . "

The stranger made a humming noise and Billie stopped. Her head hurt. She looked around warily. The stranger was still lying face down in the mud. The aircar was still smoking. Harmer was not in sight. His crossbow was on the ground beside the stranger. She got up shakily and moved over to the stranger. She saw the flap of skull and the letters TFM on the side of his neck.

"Artificial," she said. She stood beside the inert figure holding the crossbow. It was light, very light, made of nanocarbon fibre. A button hid under a finger guard on the end of the stock. She pressed it and the crossbow reverted to the walking stick. The bolt fell to the ground.

"Slick," she said and bent over to pick up the bolt just as Harmer came around from behind the aircar, his face a rictus of anguish. He saw Billie and froze in an attitude of dread and disbelief.

"You were dead. I killed you," he stammered.

Billie looked up casually, noticing he had reverted to his pure black skin. "Yeah. That's right."

"What are you? Some kind of zombie?" Terror etched his face.

Billie squeezed and prodded the staff trying to make it revert to a crossbow. She wanted to keep the conversation going while she got the crossbow ready. "No. I'm just a normal person who has been treated with Restart. It keeps a molecular snapshot of my body at this age, and when I die, it restarts me."

The Kid absorbed this information without comment while watching her fiddle with the staff. Billie caught two knobs on the top end and the staff shapeshifted to a grey carbon ball, a little larger than the drone ball.

"It's on the end, but three sides," said Harmer trying to be helpful.

Billie squeezed the ball, got a staff, and looked at the end. A third knob projected on the front. When she pressed all three, the staff shifted into a crossbow. She started fitting the bolt and then stopped. Harmer was not presently dangerous. She stood facing him with the bolt in one hand and the crossbow in the other.

"Why did you shoot me?" she demanded.

"I had to remove the danger. He had something in his hand." Harmer pointed to the prostrate stranger. "It happens without thinking." It all came out in a rush.

Billie didn't quite know what to think. She had not seen anything in the man's hand. The android, the robot, she was at a loss just what to call the silver stranger. She edged over beside him. A small oval object lay under the right hand. She picked it up and examined it. It was tear-shaped, like a model of the aircar, with no markings.

Harmer approached her as she knelt beside the android. "See. I was right."

"About that, yes," said Billie, "but that still does not tell me why you shot me."

Harmer said nothing.

"Help me move him." Billie set the crossbow aside, and held on to the bolt and the tear-shaped oval. She pressed the flap of skull back in to place and it seemed to stick. She turned the robot over and tugged him into a sitting position, pulling an arm across her shoulders. "Here. Grab his other arm."

Harmer seemed to have developed a new found respect for her. He jumped to obey. Together, Billie and Harmer pulled, half-dragging the stranger out of the mud onto the north bank of the gully. They laid him on his back. He was breathing lightly, but had no pulse. The body armour looked like a crystal web across his front, except it was quite solid. Billie rummaged through her belt pouch for a crystal of Reclaim. She found one and headed back to the smoking craft.

"What are you doing? That thing could blow up anytime. And there might be more of them. We need to get away from here." He was starting to get agitated again.

"I know. Calm down," said Billie, continuing towards the craft. Harmer watched from the lip of the gully as Billie walked around the crash. She tossed the stranger's oval object into the smoking interior, then moved to the front. She held a Reclaim crystal over the flattened wing surface, squeezed and pressed. The pieces fell on the wing and Billie stepped back. At first nothing seemed to happen, then a flurry of motion swept outward from where the crystal had landed. As the tiny robots replicated and disassembled the metal, the whole craft moved and seethed. The wing appeared to dissolve inwardly. A funnel of black motes, the tell tale whirlwind of Reclaim dots spiralled overhead arcing towards the north. The whole ship was quickly dissolved and, in a couple of minutes, was gone.

Harmer stood aghast, when Billie ambled back toward him. "That is military nano."

"No. That is Finian's nano. He makes and programs it. It's called Reclaim." She turned and looked pointedly at Harmer. "Don't be too quick to judge when you don't know."

Harmer was speechless, which suited Billie just fine. She stopped at the still unconscious form of the stranger. She noted the name on the side of his neck. "TFM, eh? As good a name as any. I hope it wakes up soon. I don't want to drag him all the way to the Mission."

"The Mission?" Harmer left the question hanging.

"Hannah will be able to help him if anybody can." Billie replied as if that answered all. "Get your things together. We're leaving."

They quickly assembled their few belongings and returned to the android. To Billie's surprise when they tried to lift the stranger, he stood by himself. She gazed at him in surprise. There was no recognition in his eyes, nobody home. The face was perfectly immobile, but he would walk when started. He never gave any other sign. In itself, it was a little spooky.

Once they had gone just a short distance, the Restart and the rest of the day seemed to catch up with Billie. She felt ill to her stomach. A wave of exhaustion wrung her. A pile of boulders sat about a kilometre from the Big Tree. "Let's stop there for a bit," she nodded toward the rocks. Harmer looked at her oddly, but said nothing. When they got there, TFM would not enter the shade of the boulders. He leaned against the south side of the rock holding his arms out. Billie collapsed on the ground on the north side out of the sun and Harmer positioned himself on the side where he could watch both Billie and TFM.

"It's using the sun for energy," said Harmer. "What do you think it is?"

Billie opened her eyes and looked at him. "I don't know. It has no pulse. It breathes. Hannah has a medscan." All at once, Billie felt like the whole world was collapsing on her. A hot flush swept her forehead. She gagged and vomited a stream of black semisolid material. She arched her back and retched again, clearing the bile from her throat.

"Oh that's better. Restart always leaves a load in your stomach." She sighed and sat back. A sip of water went down easily and she did not feel nauseous any longer. "Just give me a couple more minutes."

Harmer fished in his pack and took out the drone ball. He launched the craft and fiddled with his heads-up display the way he always did. "I'd better keep an eye out in case there are more where he came from," he said. TFM had closed his eyes. Leaning spread eagled against the hot boulder, he soaked up the sun's rays.

Billie stood. "The Mission is about six days, in that direction. There's lots of water. Let's go." As she walked, it occurred to Billie that she had not wanted to take Harmer near any of the People, but now the stranger had made that unavoidable.

Evidently Harmer was fascinated by Restart because he kept coming over and asking Billie questions about different aspects of the nanotech as they walked. A steady wind blew from the southwest — hot and dry. There was nothing to do but set a slow and steady pace and keep going. The only problem with

Harmer's curiosity was that it made her open her mouth. She didn't like getting dirt on her teeth.

One time Harmer wandered over beside Billie and asked, "What's it like?"

"What is what like?"

"What's it like to die?"

Billie sighed and glanced at him sideways. How could she explain this skein of circumstance is all that is? Embrace it, foster it and be glad. Harmer's dread curiosity was behind his new found fear and respect for her. It was the kind of question only the inexperienced would ask. It was equally a driving force in the dead god religions of the Old Ones. There was no simple and straightforward way to answer. She shrugged. "It hurts. There is nothing. It's like waking up and being eighteen again."

"Nothing?"

"Nothing," affirmed Billie.

Harmer drifted away looking more puzzled than ever.

Another time Harmer approached and asked, "Do you remember everything?"

Billie answered, "It depends. The nano preserves the long term memories if it can, but it can't do much about the short term memories. Sometimes you don't remember a few minutes just before you die. It depends."

Harmer looked at her perplexed, "Depends on what?"

"I'm not sure." said Billie. "It has something to do with how quickly the short-term memories are converted into long-term, how significant the events seem to your back brain." Harmer was still frowning, so Billie tried another tack. "Have you ever known an epileptic?"

Harmer shook his head. "No, but I've been hit by a neural field that causes seizures."

"It's a little bit like that. Sometimes epileptics remember more or less what they were doing; sometimes they don't."

Harmer nodded. "There was a guy in our platoon. He's dead now." He ducked his head momentarily. "He used to say the ancients called it being touched by god."

Billie nodded, looking at the land ahead. "So I've heard."

Harmer stopped and looked at her intently. "Do you think there are some thoughts, some experiences, the mind can't deal with, like being touched by god, which make it rebel and seize?"

Now Billie stopped and looked back at him. "No. I think the epileptic has a problem in brain chemistry. The brain spins mind and reality. Things like epilepsy and Restart just cut a cross section through the illusion for a moment and remind you what's going on."

"What about your soul?"

Billie shook her head. "I bet you believe in the little man in the radio too."

Harmer frowned, but was silent.

Billie took pity and tried to explain. "People tend to see themselves in things they don't understand, like the mind or the universe. They anthropomorphize. Soul and spirit are ultimately the little man in your head because people could not understand how feelings, ideas, art and genius, all those grand conceptions could arise from a tangle of neurons."

Harmer was still silent.

"It's like the old religions. We live in this miracle." Billie spun her arm around the horizon. "And people go and put an alpha male above it all because they couldn't understand how it could run itself. The notion of a personal god is defunct since Restart. No more protection racket."

Harmer either didn't understand or care what Billie meant and busied himself with the drone's heads-up display. Later in the day he sidled over to Billie and asked, "What happens if you die somewhere you can't Restart alive? Say if you get trapped underwater?"

Billie nodded. "It's called the Living Death. It scares some people. You'll notice they don't like to be alone much." She paused. "You have a choice during the initiation preparations. Your Restart can be programmed so that if you die so many times in an hour, it quits."

Harmer studied her face. "And what about you?" he asked.

Billie grimaced. "No limit. I've always been independent. 'Born naturally cussed' my daddy used to say."

"You knew your parents?"

"Yeah. They've been gone a long time." Billie turned away.

"Gone?"

"Yeah."

"What happened to them?" Harmer persisted in spite of Billie's evident reluctance to talk.

"They disappeared. I came home one day, supper was on the table and they were gone." Billie hurried to catch up with TFM who was drifting ahead on a stretch of firm ground.

A couple of hours later, Harmer was back with another question. "What happens if somebody decides they don't want to Restart? They want to stop."

Billie shrugged. "It's too late then. The time to make that decision is before the initiation. Some do decide that."

This was obviously not what Harmer wanted to hear. A wide frown creased his face. "But how can you know then?" he asked.

Billie stopped walking and turned to face Harmer. TFM was having a rough time in loose sand, so she had a moment. "We can't always. But we try. That is the purpose of the initiation leading up to the time of the Restart imprint. You only do that after your vision quest." She paused momentarily and chuckled. "Of course, in a sense your vision quest never ends, but you have to know your tribe and your work to make the decision."

Harmer did not look any happier. It may have been that he did not understand at all what she was talking about, so Billie told him a children's campfire story. "One guy, before I was born, tried to commit suicide." That caught Harmer's attention. "He went into a kind of frenzy, playing with death. He kept shooting himself and Restarting.

Harmer looked properly awestruck and asked "So what happened?"

"One of the elders shot him." Billie paused and caught his eye. "In the head." Harmer didn't get it, so Billie explained. "The Restart nano won't touch the brain unless there is severe trauma. It fixes veins and skull and stuff, but leaves the neurons alone; it leaves the mind alone. So by shooting him in the head, the elder made the Restart rebuild the brain completely. He came out of it with the mind and memories from just before his initiation at age eighteen."

Harmer looked a little stunned, but Billie continued blithely, "Of course, that was only the immediate problem. After a lot of discussion in the lodge, the consensus was he needed to grow differently, in a new social matrix. He needed to leave the village."

Harmer looked at Billie blankly and started to drift away. He wasn't uncomfortable; he simply seemed to have no grasp of social context.

Billie let her train of thought finish pulling into the station, anyway. "They say he is quite different now. You'll probably meet him. Goes by the name Jorge, now."

Harmer's final question to Billie about Restart was perhaps predictable. "Can I use Restart?"

Billie nodded and started to explain. "Like I said, there is an initiation. You need to go on your vision quest. You need to know your tribe and choose a work. It helps if you have been tested."

"Tested?"

Billie nodded. "By circumstance."

Harmer frowned. "And what if I don't want all that stuff, I just want the Restart?"

Billie shook her head. "The lodge would never agree. The imprint needs to be tailored for you, so you need their sanction and their help."

Harmer looked furious. His skin started to change to camouflage colouration. He visibly shook himself and walked stiffly away. Billie watched this reaction thinking, well, we have got a little beyond the idiotic grin. What would ever become of this angry and excitable boy?

✦

With the steady metronomic pace set by TFM, the trip to the Mission took only four days, two nights without water. TFM slowed down a lot when the sun was not shining, but when it was, he was relentless.

The Mission was not visible from afar, because, even though it was three stories high, it sat in a shallow valley only just coming even with the surrounding country. Billie knew the district well and led them into the southern end of the garden valley. A couple of hours later, they rounded a bend and there, nestled among trees, not more than two kilometres away, was the Mission settlement — four or five small wooden houses and the squat stone structure itself — in the middle of an irrigated green swath. Because Hannah was a Seedkeeper, she endeavoured to have as much greenery and plant life around her as possible. The fields and gardens lined with trees were testament to that, but the limiting factor was, as always, water.

The Mission walls were sandstone and Billie remembered working her way around them looking for fossils in the stone — trilobites and ammonites. The building had survived since the time of the Old Ones; had once been a municipal building; now Hannah had taken it over.

As long as Billie could remember, she had heard about Hannah. Her tribe was healer and her work was caring for the children. She was the good-hearted, crazy old woman who lived on the outer reaches and took care of the genetically flawed, the malformed and simple-minded children, who were a legacy of the biowar.

Hannah had come to Restart late in life, so she always looked old. Once in a fit of curiosity, Billie had asked Hannah why she hid herself out in the southern wastes. Hannah had smiled gently like she was talking to a child, and replied, "My children are all dead in the war. I cannot help them, but I can help these who nobody else wants. Children have a capacity for joy that is infinitely refreshing." And that was all she had said. Billie found that the phrase "a capacity for joy" echoed in her mind's ear more than once.

Some in the village had a jaundiced view of Hannah. She was a study in tough love. She had been military and espoused the doctrine of original integrity a little too fearlessly for the taste of some. She was apt to veer into philosophical discussion a little too easily when asked a simple question. It is all too easy to upset folks who do not want to be disturbed, who do not want to move past a certain style of life and thought. The People were pragmatic. They appreciated the wise ones among them, but they had a long history of cultural oppression and prejudice, and they were not about to let some near Old One tell them what to think or believe. Of course, most of those who spoke this way had never been near the Mission, still that was the attitude.

Now, on approaching the front steps of the Mission and seeing Hannah standing there by the door, Billie's first thought was how old she was starting to look. She was grey, and harried looking, a large brown-skinned matronly queen bee of a woman who used humour to maintain control. Her perpetual bustling air seemed to have wound down.

Hannah's face was beaming as her eyes fixed on Billie. "Well Billie, you look younger," she said in greeting.

"Yes, I am," replied Billie glancing at Harmer. Hannah caught the look and stepped back. She eyed the black stranger speculatively for a moment then turned to take in TFM standing motionless by the stairs.

A grey shriveled up character beside Hannah mused, "Well, well, well. What do we have here?"

"Oh Jorge, get out of the way," said Hannah in some affectionate exasperation. "Shouldn't you be upstairs for shift change?" Jorge ducked his head and disappeared inside. Hannah turned back to TFM.

"Can you speak?" she asked. TFM gave no indication it was aware of her, let alone of anything she said.

"Where did you find this?" Billie and Harmer both stepped back as Hannah walked around the android, examining him. Her breath caught in her throat when she saw the letters imprinted on the side of his neck.

"He was in an aircar that crashed down along Last Bush," Billie offered.

Hannah raised an eyebrow. "Bring him inside to Diagnostics. We'll see what the medscan can tell us."

TFM seemed baffled by the stairs, and Billie and Harmer had to help him, one leg at a time, up the short flight. Inside Hannah led them though a front lobby, down a hall and finally into a medical room. It was about six by twelve metres with a high ceiling and a high southern facing window. A side door at the other end of room led down to the basement, Billie remembered. The afternoon sun cast a bright rectangle of light on the tile floor.

"Put him up on the gurney, there," Hannah pointed, as she looked through a cupboard at the other end of the room. Billie and Harmer walked him over to the stretcher. Billie pushed a small stool in front of it for him. TFM just stood there, so Billie turned him and guided him until he was sitting on the edge. Hannah approached TFM with a small hand scanner. As she walked she bumped into a small table hitting an instrument. Harmer caught it as it was falling and put it back on the table all in one smooth motion. Hannah ran the probe back and forth across TFM's chest while reading the scanner. Billie stepped back.

Harmer went to the door and turned. "I'm going to take a look around," he said and ducked back into the hallway. Already in their brief time indoors, he had started to whiten, Billie noticed.

"Lay down," said Hannah to TFM, but he did not move. She set the scanner probe down and lifted TFM's legs while turning his upper body and laying him flat.

"Sparkling companion you have here," she said to Billie out of the side of her mouth. She scanned TFM's the entire length.

"The side of his skull was cracked open a little," said Billie.

"Where?"

"Above the right ear."

Hannah rotated TFM's head and tested the side of the skull gently with a metal probe. With a snick, a section of skull folded neatly sideways.

"It wasn't like that," said Billie.

"Well," said Hannah. "Let's take a look. Help me roll him." The two women wrestled the gurney over to a large sideways U-shaped device. The table just fit evenly between the arms.

"Step back," said Hannah as she went to the control console. A loud hum filled the air as current flowed into a large superconducting magnet. The U-shaped medscan slid down to TFM's feet. Slowly it progressed up the body toward the head. When the U-shape reached TFM's waist, abruptly everything stopped. The lights went out.

"Damn!" said Hannah in the half-lit room. "Now what?"

TFM's head began to glow. His crown shimmered momentarily with a golden halo. It looked like wild nano was about to erupt. Billie darted to the door, then looked back to see where Hannah was. She had stopped on the way to the door and was watching TFM. A shimmering band of light about three centimetres wide was progressing down his body. The band extinguished at the feet and the body jolted once. Violently. The section of skull closed seamlessly with a distinct click.

TFM moaned."Unnnh."

Billie and Hannah stood rooted watching TFM. Emergency lights came on in the room and out in the hallway. Billie moved over beside Hannah and put her hand on her shoulder.

TFM sat up at the waist, looked at the two women and said slowly and distinctly, "Thank you for resetting me. Repair functions are underway." He lay back down.

"You're welcome." said Hannah somewhat emptily. "I wonder what . . ." She stopped and pointed to TFM's feet. Growing from the bottom of his feet were a mass of carbon black fibres. They reached across the room like crystals growing in fast forward, reaching toward the rectangle of sunlight on the floor where they spread into a jet black carpet.

TFM spoke in the same slow distinct manner. "This unit will function adequately soon." Then he turned his head and said with sudden urgency, "I cannot hear The One The Many." The person was extinguished like a light. His eyes closed, his breathing became slow and regular. It was like he fell instantly asleep. Only the black nanocarbon moved, following the sunlight across the floor.

Hannah looked at Billie and chuckled. "So what do you know about your other new friend there?" She nodded toward the hallway.

Billie shook her head. "Not much. He says he came out of the badlands. Hasn't got a name, although he used to be called Harmer."

"What?!" Hannah interrupted. "I knew he had the profile, but I never dreamed you would bring a Harmer here!" she hissed vehemently. Turning to the hallway, she called "Jorge, Jorge." There was no answer. "Now where in the hell can he have got himself to?" she muttered half under her breath.

The side door to the basement at the other end of the room opened and old Jorge shuffled out, a slightly sheepish look on his face. He had been eavesdropping, Billie surmised.

"Oh there you are. Good. Jorge that black boy is a Harmer."

The old man's eyes went wide.

"I don't know what grade, but I don't want him near the children. Do you understand?"

"I hear and I obey, oh mistress of my heart." Hannah's mouth snapped shut and Billie snickered. Jorge winked at Billie on Hannah's blind side as he trundled out of the room.

"Oh and please see what's up with the power," Hannah called after him, then turned to Billie. "I couldn't run this place without him, but sometimes he pushes it." She paused contemplatively. "We tell ourselves there are no slaves and masters, no bosses, but somehow only some take responsibility. Jorge keeps me from taking it all too seriously."

Hannah suddenly changed gears. "Now! Why don't you go and get yourself settled in. I've got to find your friend." Hannah poked through several cupboards, finding an air syringe and an ampoule of medication. She bustled out of the room, leaving Billie watching the sleeping TFM. She'll never change, thought Billie affectionately, always busy, doing three things at once, and yes, always trying to run other people's lives.

◆

It did not take Hannah long to find Harmer. She knew he would be calculating defensive capabilities, so she went to the roof, and there he was, a pale white ghost studying the valley and district.

"Hello young man," she said equably, not approaching too closely, but standing to one side and peering out at the valley, as was he.

"Billie tells me you came out of the badlands," said Hannah conversationally.

Harmer did not reply.

"I'm curious," continued Hannah, "how did you deal with the heat, no water?"

Harmer scrutinized Hannah who continued looking at the valley, apparently oblivious. "I have a desert suit."

Hannah looked at him, smiled, then looked away. "There can't be much to eat down there." She left the statement hanging.

"There's food. If you know where to look."

Hannah continued as though he had not said anything "And the temperature must be a killer."

Harmer turned and held out his arm. "My skin," he said. "I can regulate my temperature."

Now Hannah turned, looking him in the face and asked quietly, "Who made you son?"

It was like touching a nerve. The reflex was triggered and Harmer snapped to attention and rapped out "Abel Tango Seven Niner Seven Number Seven reporting for duty. Sir!" He shouted the sir and held the pose, then appeared to hear the actual question and replied "You did, Sir. Thank you, Sir."

A look of disorientation passed over Harmer's face and he looked around. His eyes settled on Hannah. "What am I doing here?"

"It's okay son, just relax. I touched some of your conditioning. It's all right. I will see you don't remember this session." She paused as Harmer looked frantically about. He was starting to change into camouflage colouration, which meant he felt threatened Hannah knew.

"What is your mission protocol?" demanded Hannah.

Harmer locked eyes and frowned. "Mission protocol?" he repeatedly blankly.

Hannah sighed and repeated the sign stimulus. "Who made you son?"

Again Harmer snapped to attention and rapped out "Abel Tango Seven Niner Seven Number Seven reporting.."

"What is your mission protocol?" Hannah interrupted insistently.

"I have no mission. Sir!" He paused and again the wild-eyed searching began. "No mission." He stopped. Looked back at Hannah sharply. "All dead. The platoon, the battalion." His face contorted. "I was wounded. The medtechs froze me . . . "

"Hold out your arm soldier," said Hannah gently. She vapojected the sedative into his triceps. "You need to rest now. Lay down over there." She pointed to a wooden bench in the middle of the rooftop garden. "Rest easy and someone will take you to barracks in a while." Harmer drifted toward the bench. Hannah stayed with him talking softly all the while. "You have done well. You need to sleep. Rest now. Lie down and let it all go."

When Harmer fell asleep, Hannah sighed deeply and went looking for Billie. Contrary to her expectations, Billie was not in the cafeteria. She was in the meditation room, but she was not meditating. Her face was tied in a knot, when Hannah entered. Billie looked up. "Why do you keep that?" She pointed to a cruel-looking cross made of broken beer bottles hanging in the middle of the wall.

"It was here when I arrived. Somehow I could not bring myself to throw it out," Hannah replied, paused, then added as an afterthought, "Think of it as the union of opposites if you prefer. The youngsters come to expect the stereotypical from us oldtimers. It pays to have a discordant symbol to make them think. Some never will anyway. So be it."

Billie looked doubtful. "Yeah, well it is a little christian," she emphasized the word, "for you though, you must admit."

"Those bottles once held alcohol," continued Hannah, ignoring Billie's dig. "The Old Ones are gone. Their religions are gone. But addiction is not. The fundamentals remain." She paused for a moment looking at the jagged cruciform. "The world is miracle enough," whispered Hannah.

Billie was becoming uneasy. They were getting close to one of Hannah's hobby horses and she did not want to get tied up in an endless debate about old belief structures. Hannah caught Billie's look and mood, and fell silent.

Billie searched for something to change the topic. "Do you think TFM will be dangerous?"

Hannah looked at her raising an eyebrow. "I don't care about the machine. If it becomes a problem, I will Reclaim it. Your other friend there is the problem." She moved towards the west door.

"Let's go out in the garden Billie. I want to talk about Harmer, and there are too many ears here." She looked significantly back toward the central hall. Billie followed Hannah out the small side door. A gravel path led through some grounds and into a small park. They sat on a rough stone seat in front of a Japanese rock and sand garden. A recirculating pump trickle fed a pool of water from the side of a large granite rock, beside the garden. The sound of running water was almost strange, exotic for Billie after being in the desert.

"What do you know about Harmer?" asked Hannah.

"Not much. Like I told you. I ran into him in the Dead City. He said he came out of the badlands."

"Are you sure he came out of the badlands?"

"Well, I followed his trail back for two days, which was about as far as I could. The wind had covered most of his tracks by then, and water was a factor."

Hannah mulled this information. "I don't understand why he should show up now," she said finally.

Billie looked puzzled. "Why? What do you mean?"

"Did you notice Harmer's reaction time?"

"No. When?"

"When I knocked that lascalpel off the desk."

"I must have been looking at TFM. Why?"

"His reaction time was fast. Very fast. He caught that thing before you or I could possibly have reacted."

Billie looked puzzled. "Yeah, so?"

"It means he is accelerated."

Billie still looked puzzled. Hannah sighed. "That's what I was afraid of. You have led a little bit of a sheltered life, Billie Featherstone."

Billie turned sharply, starting to get angry. "Now look. I have been a Ranger for over a hundred years." She jumped up and stomped back and forth in front of Hannah. "If it walks or flies, I've seen it. If it's edible, I have hunted and killed it. There is not much in this land that I have not seen or done."

Hannah sat quietly and listened, letting the angry words flow away. Abruptly Billie sat down. They sat in silence for a minute.

"I agree that you know our lands inside and out," Hannah started. "But there is a whole world out there you have never seen. All the lost lands."

Again silence stretched between them. Billie was calming down but her heart still pounded. At the far end of the park, a swirl of sparrows twittered and darted.

"Did I ever tell you how I came to the People?" Hannah asked.

Billie shook her head.

"I was a medtech in the last war." Billie was startled by the revelation that Hannah was that old. It meant her chronological age had to be over three hundred and fifty.

"We were ambushed. Slaughtered. The whole battalion was killed or captured. And not many of us were left alive. They took us underground in some camp and chained us to pipes. I think at that point we were a long-term food supply. It was right at the end of the fall and things were pretty grim."

Billie stared at Hannah in stunned silence.

"We were chained there for six or seven days. It was hard to tell. I kept passing out. I was wounded. Something must have happened to the mob that captured us, cause the camp went silent. We were alone in the dark. I was preparing to die. We had no food, a little water. I couldn't do a thing. By this time I was half-crazy, I suppose. Delirious." She let the word hang, and paused, listening to a raven screech down the valley.

"Then I heard singing. And this line of rough looking natives filed into the room chanting. I thought I was hallucinating, but they set me free. It was the first Rangers from Big Sky, although at that time I didn't know who they were. I didn't care as long as I got free."

Hannah stopped and stared into the distance. Billie could see how difficult it was for her to relive these events. "I came back to the village with them. It was before Restart. Finian had not shown up yet. I made myself useful with my medtech training, but a lot of people were dying. Most of those who rescued me are gone now. Old Lester. Old Lester who said the white man was Windigo."

Billie wondered why Hannah was telling her this story, when Hannah tuned in to her. "Billie there is a whole world outside these lands that you have never seen. I know your age and I know you study during the winter, but . . ." she stopped and changed tack. "There were killing things made during the war that you could scarce imagine." She gazed intently at Billie. "Your friend there is one of them."

"He's not my friend," Billie retorted.

"Whatever!" Hannah snapped. "He's a genmod soldier, created for the desert. He's accelerated. His reaction time is ten times faster than yours or mine. His nervous system is tuned by a combination of bioengineering and drug generating implants. He has genmod eyes that can see into the infrared and probably other genmod senses as well. He lives mostly on photosynthesis. He is capable of extreme violence in the wink of an eye. He will just automatically calculate half a dozen ways to kill anyone within ten metres. I saw what they did in my unit. Believe me, you don't want to mess with them."

Billie stared open-mouthed. Was this what she had brought to the People?

"Our one stroke of luck is that he is not in combat mode. He is not currently on a mission."

Billie absorbed this information in silence. She raised her eyes to look at Hannah.

"What did you think you were going to do with him anyway?"

Billie shrugged. "When I found him, I didn't know what to think. I didn't believe his story about coming out of the badlands, but where else could he be from? I didn't know what to think, so I decided to take him with me, to learn more about him before deciding."

"And what would you do if you found out he was lying?" Hannah asked.

Billie shook her head. She was feeling bad. She felt foolish. Her lack of knowledge had proven dangerous. "Worst case? I'd have had to kill him I guess."

Now Hannah shook her head. "He will never knowingly put himself in danger and he would certainly kill you if you did anything hostile."

"He already did," said Billie with a wry grimace.

"Ah yes. I thought that's what you meant."

Billie was thoughtful as Hannah groped for explanations. "For him it is not a matter of right or wrong; nothing to do with morality or ethics. He is conditioned. He simply does what the world allows and what his conditioning demands."

Billie frowned as Hannah continued. "There is another thing too. Don't let it fool you. He had no childhood. His childhood memories are completely artificial."

A curious expression played across Billie's face. "Does he know that?"

Hannah shook her head. "Rarely do they know. He may know something is not quite right, but he won't really know what it is."

"What can we do?" Billie asked. Hannah did not answer and together they sat gazing at the rock garden, listening to the birds and the trickling water. "Is it possible to decondition a Harmer?"

This made Hannah stop and think. "Maybe, I don't know. It is certainly possible to disable his implants." She looked at Billie. "I never knew the command protocols, only the medical. A full and proper deconditioning would require his cooperation."

A squabble of sparrows alighted in the branches overhead and they both looked up. "Do you think he would be interested?" asked Hannah.

"I don't know," Billie replied.

"Well that is something to think about, something to find out." Hannah turned and looked to the west. "It's getting late. Did you know that Cookie has a big spread planned for the evening meal? We don't get many visitors. Everyone will be there." Side by side the two women walked slowly back toward the Mission. The setting sun bathed the old stone building in a rich red gold light.

The Machine City

Net primary production:
"Net primary productivity [NPP] is the total energy trapped in photosynthesis worldwide, minus what is required by the plants themselves, or in slightly more technical terms, the total chemical energy produced by chemoautotrophic and photoautotrophic organisms less the energy they use in respiration. NPP is sensitive to all of the factors controlling primary productivity such as climate, carbon dioxide, water, fertilization, desertification and land use. The percentage of NPP appropriated by humans can be used as an index of their impact on the biosphere. By the start of the third millennium, the percentage was estimated to be 40% and increasing."
— Encyclopedia Solaris [2443 OT Edition]

✦

EARLY THE NEXT MORNING, Billie got up and went looking for something hot to drink. To her surprise Cookie was in the kitchen already preparing breakfast. She waved to him stirring a large steaming pot in the back, grabbed a mug of hot tea and went up to the roof to watch the sun rise. The valley was dark. Golden violet fingers of cloud reached across the eastern sky.

Behind her the door to the patio opened and Hannah came out. "Morning."

"Hello. How are you? Sleep well?"

"Yes, fine thanks." Billie felt a little ritualistic. She was unused to being around people. She sighed and let the feeling pass.

Billie pointed north past the end of the cultivated area, where a work site was just becoming visible in the growing light.

"I was trying to make out what that is."

Hannah glanced and chuckled. "It started as a simple project. We wanted to drop a second well. For the north end gardens and as a backup in case this one . . . " She nodded to the closer pump house. "Well, just in case . . . "

Billie nodded.

"The water table here is about forty metres. So we started drilling and ran into something concrete. We punched through the top and damned if it wasn't an old hazardous materials dump. All this time, we'd never even known it was there." Hannah shook her head and stared at the horizon contemplating the possibilities.

"So anyway, we opened it up and Reclaimed a bunch of gunk. Then we hit a section of low level radioactives." Hannah sighed. "We couldn't Reclaim that so we poured sand in it and sealed it. We'll have to drill somewhere else," she finished resignedly.

Billie shook her head in disgust. "Damn them anyway."

Hannah raised an eye.

"The Old Ones."

Hannah skewered Billie with a look. "You may curse them, but do not think you are all that different. They were just people, like you and me, trapped in a situation beyond their control."

"But the wasting . . . "Billie gestured to the desolate land beyond the valley.

"I know. I know. The world is in ruins and you blame. It's so easy, so tempting and so useless. It absolves all responsibility and leaves you nowhere."

Billie stared at her suddenly vehement friend.

"Look here is something for you to consider," said Hannah. "If you lived a thousand years ago, what would you have done? Would you have been any different? Think about it. Humans all over the solar system. Everything run by the corporations. Every breath you take, everything you do and say monitored."

Hannah paused and Billie said nothing. Half a dozen sparrows flew overhead twittering and tussling. Below them on the ground, Harmer strolled out the front door of the Mission and went around the back to the park. They watched him go in silence.

"We are no different flesh. The Old Ones were trapped, consumed by systems they could barely understand or control. We need to do something different. We need to make better people." All at once Billie saw what was behind Hannah's statement — her belief in original integrity. For her, the past was not a curse.

"The People are strong," said Hannah, suddenly changing gears and grinning, "well, because of Restart, but they are also strong because we are a community. The Great Lodge binds and guides us. Do you think that will last when there are a million of us? What stories, what elders will guide us, when we are a million?"

"The land will not support that many," Billie replied with a frown.

For a moment Hannah looked thoughtful. "Now there is a question for you to take back to the lodge. What is the optimal number of humans on the planet?"

Billie shrugged. "For what? According to whom? Any answer you might give has an implicit value judgment. What do you want to maximize? The number of dogs? The stability of the ecosystem? There are always winners and losers."

This was an old argument the women had visited many times in the past and they both recognized it. "Honestly, Hannah, sometimes you talk the sheerest nonsense." Hannah always argued for critical analysis, preferably numeric. If you can't measure it, it doesn't matter. And Billie always argued the morality of a people living in harmony with their world.

"No Billie, that is not how it works. It doesn't matter a damn what you think or believe. You have to eat, that is all. It all comes down to energy flows, predator and prey numbers, the consumer and producer characteristics. Personal belief does not matter." Hannah paused dramatically and looked at Billie in a sudden silence. "There is an awful lot of holier-than-thou-mumbo-jumbo passed off as understanding. The next time you hear somebody making pronouncements about 'living in harmony', ask them how they measure that. Sometimes you need a scalpel to cut through the crap."

Billie was not going to be cowed by mere vehemence. "Okay Hannah, here is something else to consider. Have you thought about how Restart changes the equation — your precious predator and prey numbers? We've knocked your numbers all askew." Billie was looking for a soft spot, but she didn't find one.

"Yes I know," Hannah replied. "That's another side of my earlier question about carrying capacity. How do we limit our population growth? What do we do with those who don't understand or who refuse to accept the necessity of limits?"

"Well we can all see how mother nature handles it," Billie waved her arm at the desert beyond the valley.

Hannah turned suddenly towards Billie. "When you find yourself in that kind of logical box, you know the rules have to change. The situation needs to be seen in another light."

Billie let herself get carried away by the rhetoric. "Oh swell. So how do we just wave our hands and make this problem go away?"

"I don't know," said Hannah quietly, "but I do know we must."

The frank admission took some of the wind out of Billie's sails. She cast about another subject. "You know, there is something else I should tell you."

Hannah looked at her sharply.

"There are some new animals."

"What?"

Billie told Hannah about the dragonfly and the strange bird. She was unimpressed.

"There's more," said Billie, and told her about the Ultra and the buffalo. That made Hannah stop and wonder.

"There's still more," said Billie, and related the incident with the dead lizard.

"You're right," Hannah concluded. "Something is going on. I'll tell Finian, so that it gets back to the lodge. I wonder what the Ultras are doing?"

The door onto the patio behind them opened and Jorge stuck his head out. "Hannah."

Hannah turned to Billie. "I've got to go. I'll talk to you later." She headed towards Jorge and then as though to précis her earlier argument, looked back over her shoulder and said, "Better people." She ducked inside talking animatedly to Jorge behind the glass.

Billie sighed and looked around the valley. That was easy to say, but what did it mean. Particularly if Hannah was right and the extinction was more about numbers than about belief structures. What else could "better people" mean? Not the Ultras, that was for sure. She peered at the drilling site to the north. The sun was shining brightly now and she could see where the ground had been opened.

TFM stepped out the front door of the Mission building below. Billie leaned over the edge and called down, "Where are you going?"

TFM looked up at her. "Home," he said and started walking back down the valley toward the south.

"Wait!" called Billie and dashed downstairs.

A couple of minutes later, Hannah returned to the roof and saw Billie running down the road after TFM. She watched them head down the valley and disappear around the bend. "Well that was short and sweet," she said aloud, shaking her head. Her stalwart friend was off chasing wild geese. Again! She headed back downstairs. "Now what do I do with that Harmer?"

An hour or so later, Hannah was in the kitchen discussing menus and schedules with Cookie, when Harmer walked in.

"Where's Billie?" he demanded, speaking over their conversation.

Hannah put her hand on the cook's arm to forestall him reacting and replied, "She followed the machine back down the valley."

Harmer turned abruptly and left. Hannah finished her business with Cookie and went back up to the roof. Harmer was already halfway down the valley towards the bend. She watched for a couple of minutes, and when he passed out of sight, went back inside humming happily.

◆

It was like walking with two people in one body, Billie soon discovered. A mechanical voice, talked about joules and coordinates and redundant failure modes, and a human voice expressed anguish at being trapped inside a machine. He was caught in something beyond his control. From time to time he woke up. He didn't know why. She quickly found herself thinking of them as the robot and the human. Every once in a while the human came to the fore and said, "I cannot hear The One The Many," with a kind of primeval horror which meant nothing to Billie.

It seemed the human component defined the direction in which the body moved. During one lucid moment, Billie asked TFM where he was going and he replied, "To the city."

Billie's heart sank. The Machine City was far to the southwest, well beyond the Last Bush. She had been there before, when she had gone to check the monolith's slow encroachment, but it was not a trip to be undertaken lightly. What was worse was that TFM would not set a sensible course. It was only with great difficulty that she got him to stop at a well. She had some fresh supplies from the Mission, but hadn't been ready for a trip. A lot of desert survival consisted of doing the right thing at the right time and TFM made that difficult. She prepared herself for a long haul.

Billie never did see Harmer, but she saw the nanocarbon drone and knew he was following. Once she caught a flicker of motion to her right where she would not have expected a follower to be, but TFM would not wait and she could not go to check for tracks. Not that it mattered much anyway, she decided, what was she going to do? Maybe it was just a wandering coyote she had seen. After what Hannah had told her, she was just as glad if Harmer followed at a distance. She was no longer quite sure just how to treat him; no longer sure what made sense as her basic emotional stance towards him. He had gained a lot of respect for her, simply because of Restart, but he was still a severely damaged individual. Above and beyond his deadly nature, he needed to be handled carefully and correctly.

Why was she following TFM? Billie was hard pressed to answer that question for herself. She was curious and afraid. She had never seen anyone or anything quite like him before and she needed to make sure the Machines were not surging. She knew there had been times when they had done that in the past. Behind her concern was a deeper curiosity — she wanted to know what the Machine City experienced. The kaleidoscopic images she had seen suggested a realm beyond anything in her life and she wanted to know.

As the days and kilometres and disjointed conversations passed, she settled into a mood of watchful curiosity. TFM rarely spoke and then it was mainly the robot reporting. He kept his sunlight hours, starting when the sun rose a hand above the horizon, and stopping at sundown. Occasionally Billie was able to arrange a decent camping spot for the night; more often they slept in the open, with no cover. TFM drank a little water, about once a week. He never ate. When they passed the Last Bush, Billie had to forcibly restrain TFM until the human appeared and she made him understand they had to travel now from well to well.

The land was a series of long shallow hills and valleys. Nothing grew. It was dust and wind, morning noon and night. The odd valley was cut with a deeper gully where there had once been a river, but there was no water anymore. They moved in a zigzag course from well to well across the land. Billie had to keep a constant eye on TFM, because left alone he would start off on a heading directly towards the Machine City, nowhere near any well.

It made a common tableau. Old abandoned buildings, ruined houses crumbling to dust; sometimes the barns and sheds were metal. They stood up well in the dryness. Old farming equipment, dead agrobots and other larger incomprehensible machines lay half-buried by sand in the old farmyards. No animals, no birds, no insects — sand and silence and the dead. Somehow it always seemed more desolate around such places and she never wanted to linger.

Billie began to notice that the human came to the fore in the evenings, after they stopped for the night, particularly if there were a fire. There is something primal about a dancing flame that captures the primitive and the aesthete alike. So it was with TFM. He seemed to enjoy the flames, and he stayed in the fore longer.

One night, as they sat beside a fire, he asked her, "Do you remember the old moon?"

Billie shook her head. "No. I've seen pictures is all."

They both turned and looked at the glassy, silver sliver floating in the southern sky.

"I can access memories of the day," he said.

"The Day with Two Suns."

"Is that what you call it? Funny name. It wasn't that bright you know. Everywhere across the hemisphere, you knew that people were looking up and seeing the colonies destroyed. It seemed to go on for a long time."

One day the human in him came forward in some distress. "I see these flashing images sometimes. Very vivid, very fast, flashing, photographic, luminously startling scenes — a magnified image of a dung beetle, a starfield, a dead dog, a cross section of an eyeball — violent, horrendous, strangely beautiful colours, but the images have no emotional context. They flash by and are quickly replaced. If I pay attention to them, they go faster and faster and I lose all touch with the world, with myself eventually."

Billie stared at TFM not knowing just how to react. It was just the way the Machine City appeared to her. Then all at once it was too late. The robot started talking about the temperature profile of a nuclear reaction, and Billie went back to staring at the fire. What was life like in the nanocity, she wondered.

Another night TFM started talking about SETI, the search for extraterrestrials. "The humans decided it wasn't practical to travel to the stars themselves. So instead they made a synchrotron like machine out near Saturn, the StarSeed Project. They created nanoprobes, accelerated them to relativistic speeds and shot them at stars all around. It's much cheaper in terms of energy to make something really small go very fast, you know. The criteria for the probes to start up were quite stringent — a G type star, an oxygen nitrogen atmosphere, liquid water, no artificial signals — but in the right conditions they would replicate and begin generating humans, genmod humans actually." He stared into the fire. "Still I imagine one of these centuries, they'll be calling home. That is our job — to listen. Funny that humans searched for signals from the stars for over a thousand years and never heard a peep. Now, the first signals we will hear, will be from other humans."

Then annoyingly, the human disappeared and the robot started talking about orbital parameters. Billie snapped, "Oh shut up!" and to her surprise, the robot did.

It seemed TFM liked to talk and think about the old humans, because they always seemed to figure in the subjects he raised during their evening talks. One night he talked about the Antarctic ice cap melting and the ensuing turmoil. Another time, he talked about the genetically engineered humans and the problems of intelligence increase. Billie wanted to know about the Machine City. "What is it like in the city?" she asked.

He turned to her in the half-dark. They had no fire that night. "It's just a city," he said. "All the lives and thoughts are there to access. There is always something new." Billie was terrified by the aura of ferocious normality.

They followed an unsteady heading, pushed one way by TFM's beeline for the Machine City and pulled the other by Billie's need for water. Billie switched to half-rations. If she was going to get back from this unplanned excursion, she needed to conserve. It got so that she was always hungry. The long days of steady exertion and hunger were wearing her down, drawing her nerves to a fine pitch. She persevered on grit. Fortunately she had adequate water.

At first Billie didn't realize the black shape she saw was the city. It was different. It wasn't moving. The Machine City looked dead. Jet black and non-iridescent it floated in the heat waves like a mirage. Towers and spires, houses and trees, roadways and vehicles all frozen in crystalline blackness. It looked like a gigantic obsidian clockwork to Billie.

"What happened to it?" she asked.

TFM came and stood beside her. "I cannot hear The One The Many."

Billie shook her head. It was late in the afternoon, but TFM did not want to wait, and Billie followed. When they approached the boundary, Billie noticed that sand had drifted onto the black nano material. TFM stared at it as if he could not believe his eyes. The human came to the fore and said, "Something is very wrong." He started into the black city. For a moment Billie hung back. The first step onto the blackness was difficult, but once nothing happened, she hastened after TFM.

A couple of hundred metres inside the city, TFM walked up to what looked like a public console built into the side of a building, and started pressing buttons. Billie was just behind him. She heard a crackling, static electricity noise. Beside the building, on her left, about twenty metres away, a creature of light appeared. It was human-shaped, human-sized and walked toward them with a distressingly normal gait. It was like a hologram, except the surface appeared to flow and move with clouds of electric charges. Internally, arcs of current flowed and danced.

TFM was unmoved. Billie whispered to him, "What is that?"

"An avatar. The city wants to talk to me."

She watched both fascinated and afraid as the presence approached. About four metres away it stopped. Slowly, majestically even, the creature bowed from the waist and stood regarding them. The being of light kept its head tilted forward so that it seemed to be deferential, always looking up. It does not see through those eyes, thought Billie, but the illusion was complete.

All at once TFM said, "Can you let the human hear?"

From the teleport a strangely female voice said, "Yes, of course, although it means slowing down to human speed."

TFM turned to Billie. "My link is damaged. I cannot fully connect, but there is no one here anyway. The city says, 'they finished and left.'"

Billie looked at the avatar. "What do you mean they finished and left?"

The avatar looked at TFM. "There is another human four hundred metres south — male, biological age, twenty-three, one-point-eight metres, titanium-inlaid skeletal structure. Do you want him to hear as well?"

"No." said Billie quickly, then she repeated "What do you mean they finished and left?"

The avatar looked down. "There was some unusual electro-magnetic activity, EMPs, which generated a series of signals not aimed at me. The time period was approximately ninety microseconds. Then the citizens started to go away. At first one, then a handful, and finally they were all gone. Except you." The avatar pointed at TFM. "They left me because they knew you had gone to see the primitives. Have you completed your task?"

"My task?" echoed TFM blankly.

"You were to tell the humans — the homo sapiens and the homo superior — about the others."

"I don't think so. I don't remember."

"You are damaged. I can fix you," said the avatar.

"Wait a minute. What others?" Billie asked. The avatar ignored her. She turned to TFM. "What others?" she repeated.

Still the avatar did not reply. It would only talk to TFM. It repeated, "I can fix you."

Billie took TFM by the arm, and pulled him around. "Ask it about the others," she said forcefully.

To Billie's dismay the robot came to the fore, and started talking about coordinate systems, frames of reference and time space dilation.

From a speaker in the teleport, a recording started to play. "Bonjour. Est-ce que n'importe qui est la? Pouvez-vous m'entendre?" A squawk of nerve-scratching radio noise burst out, then it switched to another language. "Hallo. Ist jemand dort? Kannen sie mich verstehen?" Then more noise and the message "Hello. Is anybody there? Can you understand to me?"

Again the radio squealed and Billie yelled at the avatar, "Oh shut that noise off."

The human in the android took Billie's hand. "They are going right by . . ." He stopped and suddenly looked at the avatar in alarm. "It's fixing me."

TFM collapsed full length on the ground. A shimmer enveloped his head. Billie jumped back startled, as a wave of seething activity moved from his head, down his body and dissipated. TFM's eyes snapped open.

"I have full access. There is a carrier, but no signal. The One The Many are gone. No. Wait. There is something else . . ."

TFM sat up abruptly and looked at Billie. "The EMPs were . . ." he said and stopped in mid-sentence. A low moan escaped his lips. "Ooohh Nnnnooo. It cannot be." His face was drawn in precisely articulated agony.

"Nnnnooo," he cried. The buzz of wild nano made Billie jump back. TFM's legs started to dissolve into the city. He leaned on his hands and they started to dissolve. Flesh and bloody polycarbons dripped from his wrists. TFM was writhing and moaning. For a second, the city flashed white. It lurched, started to rumble and move. A beam of coherent white light arced from TFM to the teleport. The avatar disappeared. A spectrum of colours radiated from the android's body as he melted into the ground. Two wild, tortured and very human eyes locked on Billie. "Vishnu is in Tsiolkovsky!" he shouted. "Run!"

Billie turned in a wild rising panic and ran for dear life. Beneath and behind her, the city stormed and flashed. A wild nano iridescence shimmered and she jumped sideways. Harmer was running ahead of her. Total and unthinking panic gripped her. The rumble and buzz of the city grew in intensity, seemed to envelope her. She ran heedlessly, blindly, utterly without thought. Lightning flashed and she leapt onto the sand. Heart pounding and with her mind locked on the image of TFM dissolving into pieces, she raced onward.

A kilometre away from the writhing city, Billie collapsed. As she lay on the sand looking back at the strobosopic metropolis, Harmer appeared and sat beside her. Slowly Billie's panic subsided. She was suddenly exhausted, wrung dry of emotion. It was getting dark, and she needed to get away. She struggled to her feet and forced herself to move. As she stumbled into the dark, she had the impression she was listening to the death throes of a massive and tragic beast.

They made camp in a sheltered gully beside some large boulders, about four kilometres away. The city was quieting down. Billie fell fast into a deep and dreamless sleep. Harmer sat and watched the black now unmoving shape, all night long.

In the morning the world had not improved. She had new worries. She was low on food and water. If they got caught by a dust storm now, she'd be in trouble. Harmer probably wouldn't care. And there was the matter of the Machine City. She wanted to know if it was as truly dead as it now seemed. She barely considered being with Harmer a danger now, she realized, thinking wryly of Hannah's warning.

On the plus side, I feel well and truly refreshed, she thought as she stood and sipped a little water looking back at the Machine City. She was hungry, but decided not to eat. Overnight the city had died. It now looked like a flat black pile of nanoslag, a looming presence. From time to time, she looked at it in disbelief.

"Did you sleep okay?" she asked Harmer.

"I kept watch," he replied without looking away from the city.

"You should have wakened me and got some sleep."

"I'm okay."

Billie wondered about his drug implants, shrugged, then turned and started walking back toward the Machine City.

"Where are you going?" called Harmer.

She stopped and looked back at him standing by the boulders. "I have to know if it is really dead."

When they got near the edge of the Machine City, the first thing Billie noticed was that the drift sand was gone. The black heap was inert. Harmer followed about twenty metres behind her, watching carefully. Billie picked up a handful of gravelly sand and threw it on the city. The spray of sand and pebbles lay unmoving where it landed. She picked up a small rock and threw it overhand about thirty metres. The rock landed with a resonant clang, but no other reaction. Billie put one foot on the edge of the blackness, then had second thoughts. She knew that when the city was active, Remove would not work on it. Once when she had tried, there had been a flurry around the fragments of thrown crystal, a shimmer as unimaginably tiny nanowars raged, but no whirlwind ever developed. The shimmer would stop, and the city go on. Now she could use it as a test.

Billie prepared a five second crystal of Remove. She looked over her shoulder to warn Harmer, but he was gone. Billie looked all around in dismay. How the hell could he disappear that quickly? She pressed and scratched start, dropping the Remove just within the city. No nanowar erupted. The Remove worked as it should — a normal flurry ensued and a whirlwind of dancing motes rose above a growing and gaping hole. Only the surface of the city was black. Reclaim scoured away material making a smooth edged almost aerodynamic cavity about four metres across. The interior was a chiaroscuro of colours and materials. It looked like a cross-section of veins and arteries, wires and tubes, an organic machine in a riot of colours, constituting the flesh and bones of the organism.

Billie was satisfied she had good news to report in the lodge. Now she had only to get back and tell it. She turned back to the rock formation where she had slept. Harmer was leaning against the rock with his eyes closed. Just like TFM, she thought of the beginning of their trek back at the Last Bush and remembered Hannah's comment about photovoltaics. A thought of the Avatar quickly followed and she gasped at the image of TFM dissolving and howling into the black city. Harmer opened his eyes.

"It's dead," said Billie.

"I don't trust nano," said Harmer.

Billie shrugged and turned toward the north. She pointed. "There is where we must go."

"Why not here?" Harmer pointed back the way they had come with TFM.

Billie shook her head. "This way is shorter." She wasn't inclined to mention her dwindling food.

✦

Without further discussion Billie and Harmer headed off towards the Last Bush. Harmer launched his drone. The sun burned down. The sou'westerlies blew continually and they moved steadily northward. Two days later, an Ultra aircar became audible behind them. Harmer brought his drone down, and they spent a hot and uncomfortable few minutes laying side by side near the top of a dusty dune. The sound faded and they did not see a thing. Eventually they picked themselves up and struck out northward once again.

In the early afternoon, an old farm windmill tower came just into view over the horizon. Billie pulled her vuscope out and gave it a quick once over. "I know this place. There is water and wood. We'll stay there overnight."

Harmer looked pointedly at the sun hanging in the western sky, but did not reply. They walked on. He left his drone aloft. Beneath the distant tower, old metal farm buildings came into view. One long narrow barn had collapsed in the middle of several smaller sheds and the remains of a farmhouse.

Wood for a fire, and practically nothing to cook thought Billie wryly. She saw no trailsign as she wandered aimlessly through the yard. She was happy just to sit in the shade of an old steel shed and drink water. At least I have lots of that she thought with a sigh. Billie started to relax. Her head nodded and she fell asleep.

Billie awoke with a jolt, when Harmer kicked her foot. She jumped up suddenly ready to fight, and then she heard it. An Ultra aircar. It was closer this time. Harmer nodded toward the sound and headed around an intervening shed. Billie grabbed her vuscope and went around the other side. The sun was low in the west. Billie felt suddenly chagrined. She had slept during the day. She knew it was because her reserves low. She had eaten little and pushed herself to keep up with TFM, but still, she knew she had to be more careful. All at once she saw the aircar about two kilometres south and moving to the west. She shrank down to the ground and focused on the vehicle. The aircar passed in and out of sight, behind and between dunes. Harmer came up from behind her.

"Twice in one day. I don't like it," she whispered.

"Can you see how many of them there are?" asked Harmer.

Billie shook her head. "The windows are not transparent." They watched the aircar disappear. For ten or fifteen long minutes they sat and watched and listened. The aircar did not return.

The shadows were getting long and Harmer was getting lighter. From time to time it still surprised Billie how quickly it could cool off in the desert. She decided to chance a small fire. She went over to the tumbledown farmhouse looking for firewood. Blowing sand had sculpted what remained of the old building into smooth aerodynamic shapes. While she was poking around in the sand, sections of fallen wall and roof, she lost sight of Harmer. She did, however, find an old aluminum pot half-buried in the dirt. She could boil water and make a little broth. Coming back to the shed, half-dragging an armful of wood, Billie noticed the now white Harmer perched on top of the windmill tower staring intently to the south.

"See anything?" she called, but he did not reply. Billie made her fire. Harmer came down and looked on disapprovingly. He still was silent. He slunk off behind the house and Billie set about boiling up her meal for the day.

The broth was strangely satisfying. At least it quieted her pangs. She was still hungry but now she was okay. It was by then quite dark. Harmer was still nervously patrolling the perimeter behind the farm sheds. From time to time he passed in and out of the circle of light. Billie sat on the ground facing the fire with the pot between her feet. I'll have to leave that in some protected place, she thought. From here, it was four days travel north to the Last Bush, in stages she knew well. Perhaps some of the rats will not yet be hibernating. She thought about the tea she could make with leaves and bark if need be. Perhaps I should take this . . .

A voice cleared its throat. Billie looked up and a fat, bald friar in brown robes stood on the other side of fire. She tried to stand, but her foot was stuck to the ground. She lost her balance and fell back.

"Be at peace, my child. For I bring you glad tidings and great joy." He took a deep breath and chanted "Aaaaaahhhhhw wwwwwoooooooommmmmmm." The noise resonated from the buildings around. Billie wondered where Harmer had gone. Her foot locked to the ground effectively immobilized her. She struggled to move it while the friar gazed at her beatifically.

"Rejoice for you will have a wondrous visitor." Just then an ember of wood burst and a spark flew through the figure. Billie saw and realized this was a hologram.

"Where are you?" she called, not even looking at the fiction. "Come out."

The friar froze in place and around the corner of the closest shed stepped a six-armed golden ultra. He was stark naked. Around his genitalia a circle of tentacles waved rhythmically. Billie's breath stopped in her throat.

"Oh my! Aren't you the clever one! Did you like my ruse, pretty one?" asked the golden Ultra preeningly. "This is your lucky day. I will introduce you to such pleasures as you can scarce imagine. It's why I was made, you know. Utter abandon will be yours."

The Ultra lifted a device in its right middle hand. He manipulated a control with his left middle hand and Billie's foot became free. She jumped up. Then suddenly both her feet froze to the ground.

"Yes. I think you will do just fine, pretty." The Ultra walked slowly in front of Billie, examining her like a lab specimen. The tentacles were waving, reaching for her and teasing his semi-flaccid member. Billie was shaking with terror and anger. He pressed her gently between her diminutive breasts. Then suddenly shoved. She fell backwards, landing hard, her legs pulling uncomfortably, stretched unnaturally. The Ultra touched his control device again and Billie's feet moved slightly. She was flat on her back with her knees bent. She strained to sit up. One of her hands stuck to the ground.

"I've been watching you, my pretty." He knelt beside her. Billie brought her free hand up and reached for the Ultra but he grabbed her with two arms and held firmly. He was surprisingly strong. The Ultra whispered with a superior smile. "We can get rid of these unnecessarily restrictive clothes." He produced a scalpel-like instrument and moved to cut her shirt. Another hand pushed her back. "I could use a drug that would fill you with mad passion, make you cry for release, but this way is so much better, don't you think?. Raw experience untrammelled by artificialities!"

The Ultra seemed to wait for an answer momentarily, and when it didn't come, he held the knife just below Billie's chin. "Now let's see what we have here." Billie stared at him in silent fury. The feelers were stroking her leg rhythmically.

"Leave her alone!" Harmer stood behind Billie between two sheds.

The Ultra looked up in stunned surprise. "You! Where did . . . "

As soon as he looked up, Harmer let fly. The bolt struck him dead in the eye. The golden creature spasmed once and fell sideways landing on his back beside Billie. He was dead. It had all happened so fast, Billie stared dumbfounded. The bolt protruded from the eye socket, leaking a clear viscous fluid.

Harmer came up to the fire, his skin in variegated light and dark camouflage colours. "Are you alright?" he asked.

Perhaps two hundred metres away, an alarm began to whoop. Lights came on all around an Ultra aircar.

"I can't move my feet," said Billie.

"We need to get away from here," said Harmer "Now!"

"I can't move my feet," repeated Billie.

Harmer stopped cold, like he had just heard her then. "What do you mean?" he hissed in a desperate whisper. The aircar continued to whoop and flash.

"It's some kind of Ultra tech. My foot is stuck to the ground. That's the control over there." Billie pointed past the dead Ultra to where the panel had fallen beside the fire.

Harmer picked up the device and fiddled with knobs and buttons. Nothing happened. "It must be keyed to him somehow." He turned away in exasperation.

"Maybe if you use his hand," suggested Billie.

Harmer gave her a quick look, then turned back to the Ultra. He moved the creature's lower left hand toward the panel. In the distance, another aircar, perhaps two, could be heard approaching. Everything began to move in slow motion for Billie. She felt trapped in a nightmare. Harmer poked the Ultra's hand at buttons trying to manipulate the fingers to turn a knob, but still nothing happened. Billie strained to move her feet. Abruptly she decided.

"Stop!" she said, but Harmer ignored her. "Leave me. Get away. Save yourself!" she commanded.

Harmer looked at her frowning. The aircars were getting closer.

"Give me the control and go. Get the hell out of here before they arrive!" she shouted waving her one free arm. The motors were getting steadily louder.

All at once Harmer threw her the device and bolted. Billie sat anchored to the ground listening to the sound of the approaching Ultras. Again the nightmarish feeling swept over her. She tried to work the control panel with her free hand, to no effect.

One of the craft landed in the yard and a large blue four-armed Ultra approached Billie. He was the tallest Ultra Billie had ever seen, wearing a kind of body armour and holding what looked like weapons — a small gun and a coiled whip. Another hand held what appeared to be a scanning device. He surveyed the scene of Billie struggling to move her feet while the golden Ultra lay dead with the bolt protruding from its eye socket. Then he looked at Billie. "I don't suppose you'd like to tell me how you did that?"

Billie was silent. She still could not move her feet. She held the control panel and stared. The Ultra raised his head and sniffed.

"Are you alone?" he demanded. Still Billie was silent.

The blue Ultra walked around the campsite, evidently scanning the environs for other life. A brown four-armed Ultra, accompanied by a couple of small flying disks, came up to him. They spoke in a high sing-song language Billie did not understand. The second Ultra went back to his aircar that rose and started a slow circle around the perimeter of the farmyard. The flying disks remained, hovering and slowly circling the campfire.

The first Ultra started going methodically from shed to shed, exploring the inside of each briefly, and then going on to the next. He came back to the fire, which was now little more than embers, talking to the other Ultra by unseen device. He still held the weapons as though he expected trouble at any moment.

"Can you speak?" he asked. He seemed to have decided he was dealing with a mute beast.

Billie looked at him defiantly.

"Ah well. The jurors can deal with you."

The Ultra reached over with his free hand and moved a control on the hand gun. Then he aimed carefully and shot her. Billie looked down at the small, stinging dart imbedded in her shoulder and lost consciousness.

Captive

Abstract:

The current massive degradation of habitat and extinction of species is taking place on a catastrophically short timescale, and their effects will fundamentally reset the future evolution of the planet's biota. The fossil record suggests that recovery of global ecosystems has required millions or even tens of millions of years. Thus, intervention by humans, the very agents of the current environmental crisis, is required for any possibility of short-term recovery or maintenance of the biota. Many current recovery efforts have deficiencies, including insufficient information on the diversity and distribution of species, ecological processes, and magnitude and interaction of threats to biodiversity (pollution, overharvesting, climate change, disruption of biogeochemical cycles, introduced or invasive species, habitat loss and fragmentation through land use, disruption of community structure in habitats, and others). A much greater and more urgently applied investment to address these deficiencies is obviously warranted. Conservation and restoration in human-dominated ecosystems must strengthen connections between human activities, such as agricultural or harvesting practices, and relevant research generated in the biological, earth, and atmospheric sciences. Certain threats to biodiversity require intensive international cooperation and input from the scientific community to mitigate their harmful effects, including climate change and alteration of global biogeochemical cycles. In a world already transformed by human activity,

*the connection between humans and the ecosystems they depend on
must frame any strategy for the recovery of the biota.*
— Michael J. Novacek and Elsa E. Cleland[2]

◆

BILLIE WOKE UP FEELING COLD. SHE was naked. She was in a
smooth cell sculpted out of some sort of polycrete. It was
seamless. She sat up on the edge of a section of raised floor
which functioned as a bed and looked around. An oddly out of
place steel barred door was set into the smooth light-pink walls.
Beyond the bars an equally seamless hallway stretched about
ten metres to another solid door. Nothing else was visible in the
hallway. The cell was longer than wide, about four metres by six.
A hole in the floor with a small sloping circle served as a toilet.
Circling the polycrete cell, a band of wall glowed with a soft
pink light. A short, wide, and open window, recessed about forty
centimetres, crossed the top of the wall above the head of the
bed. It made a small ledge. There was absolutely nothing loose,
nothing separate she could use as a tool or a weapon.

The bed was less than two metres long, built for humans, not
Ultras. Billie shivered and goosebumps rose along her arms. She
had marks along the inside of her forearms which she couldn't
account for. A sense of disquiet crept over her as she looked at her
arms. What had happened to her? Billie rose and paced the cell.
She felt strangely detached, as though she were watching herself

[2] "The current biodiversity extinction event: Scenarios for mitigation and recovery"
by Michael J. Novacek and Elsa E. Cleland
PNAS 2001 98: 5466-5470.
Copyright (2001) National Academy of Sciences, U.S.A.
URL: http://www.pnas.org/cgi/content/abstract/98/10/5466

in a video. Why do I not feel angry? It must be the drug from that dart, she decided. She rubbed her shoulder where it had hit. There was no mark. That Ultra bastard shot me, she thought angrily. Why is there no mark? Her thoughts and feelings drifted away. She was staring dreamily at the pink polycrete light band. She scratched her head. Now that was funny.

Billie focused on the Machine City. She had been so scared when she ran. She thought of Harmer's "Leave her alone!" Her heart gave a kick and she floated away in a pink haze. This time she caught herself. If I cannot even control my own emotions, she thought. That made her stop. I cannot control my own mind. She started to get upset, took a couple of deep breaths and found herself staring dreamily at the light strip again.

Well, she thought, at least I can think. No matter what those bastards have done to control my emotions. Billie stood on the end of the concrete bed and peered out the strip of window. She could see a couple of distant peaks, with part of the side of another mountain much closer. Slabs of layered rock rose sharply. One of the distant peaks had snow. It shone a ruddy gold in the setting sun's light. Wait a minute. Is that sun rising or setting? She suddenly realized she didn't know her directions and felt completely disoriented. A wave of vertigo passed through her and she closed her eyes and leaned her forehead against the wall. How long was I out? she wondered. What have those bastards done to me?

I can tell by whether it gets darker or lighter, she decided. Assuming that this window is real and not some damned Ultra trick. She suddenly did not know what to believe or think. The cool air felt real. An odd smell of wet rock wafted from outside. It reminded her of caves she had explored. Billie thought of the Ultra shooting her, and got angry again. A wave of nausea passed through her and she jumped down from the concrete bed. She noticed this time when she started to drift away in the pink light band and purposefully pulled back to pacing back and forth with her eyes down. In a while, she climbed back up on the raised section to peer out the window. It was definitely getting darker. I want to memorize those peaks, every crook and cranny, so I will be able to recognize this place, she thought. She studied the distant cliffs intently.

Beside one of the mountains, a distant star twinkled. Billie stared at it and wondered. I am only redirected, suppressed when something touches my primitive emotions, she thought. How have those bastards done that? She started playing with her nervous system to uncover how she had been conditioned. She thought of the golden Ultra staring in amazement "Where did you come from?" She replayed the scene in her mind's eye. It was like he recognized Harmer. The image of the golden Ultra flat on its back with the bolt protruding from its eye flashed through Billie's mind and she laughed harshly. A spasm of nausea ran over her. Her shoulders heaved. She darted for the hole in the floor and made it just in time to retch. The burning acrid stomach acids filled her nose and throat. She heaved uncontrollably, gasping to breathe. A flush, a wave of heat, and then of cold, passed over her body starting from the top of her head and moving down. Raising goosebumps followed. It left her feeling cold and weak.

Billie thought again of the dead Ultra and again her whole body shook. But this time her stomach was empty. The spasms hurt. Slowly the involuntary contractions died down. Well, I have been eating anyway, she thought wryly as she leaned back against the wall, however long I may have been locked up here and even if I don't recognize what I ate. The wall was cold but she ignored it. Perhaps my thoughts are not so free after all, she mused.

The light band above her head flickered once and dimmed. Billie was not sleepy. She pushed away from the wall and started pacing. It was dark outside. I have been conditioned not to harm Ultras, Billie thought. I wonder what else? She thought of the rats she had snared. Nothing happened. Involuntarily she remembered James the elder who refused Restart, who every year explained the People's need to Grandfather Squirrel and asked permission to take some of his children. It seems the Ultras do not care if I kill animals, Billie surmised. She thought of the dead Ultra again without meaning to and spent another couple of minutes with the dry heaves.

I must learn how close I can skate to the trigger thoughts. Billie deliberately thought of the time she had found the neighbour child dead in Finian's warehouse, only his arm protruding from the pile of steel ingots that had rolled on him. She did not enjoy the memory, but she did not feel nauseous.

Then like a thunderclap it occurred to her. They do not have Restart! Dead is dead. That is why they have gone to all this trouble. Again Billie felt her gorge rise and she consciously stared at the band of light to let it soothe her. She did not vomit.

When Billie started pacing again, she suddenly remembered seeing pictures of the fabulous creatures that had once existed — large cats pacing endlessly back and forth before a crowd of people. I wonder who is watching me, she thought and started examining the walls more closely as she paced. She got so she could do it with her eyes closed. Five paces. Stop. Put out your hand and the wall was twenty-five centimetres away. She scowled and paced. Across the rooms was three paces and the wall was closer when she opened her eyes. Scowl and pace.

It was getting cold. Billie could feel cool air from the window. She shivered and rubbed her arms. A click in the hallway alerted Billie to move to the far end of the cell with her back to the wall. A brown, four-armed Ultra with a scar on his right cheek opened the far door. He was carrying her clothes — shirt, pants, underclothes and a blanket, no shoes. He had a bored officious look about him. Beside the cell door he stopped and twiddled with a control on his belt. A cabinet door flowed open in the wall and he put the clothes and blanket inside. He touched the control again and the wall flowed shut. A moment later the cabinet flowed open inside the cell. Billie approached and took the items from the recess. The Ultra manipulated his control again, and the wall flowed back to its original shape. The brown Ultra turned and left, still without speaking.

How in the hell does that work? Billie wondered. She ran her hands over the wall and felt nothing remarkable. Well it's not polycrete, she thought. I'll have to tell Finian about that. She quickly put on her clothes and wrapped the blanket around her shoulders. She was glad to be warm, even if it did mean someone was monitoring her more closely than she liked. Once again she started pacing. Slowly her scowl faded leaving only determination.

◆

After spending the night pacing and thinking, Billie was in no mood to appreciate the view from her window. The world outside slowly brightened. She spent some time watching shadows grow to determine the sun's arc. It bothered her not knowing exactly where she was. In her own territory, on her run, back out in the desert, she always knew where she was, just where the Village lay. Now she knew only her directions.

The click and clatter of the door at the end of the hallway being opened roused her. A different brown-skinned Ultra came up to the steel bars with a tray. He deposited three bulbs in the flowing wall cavity, saw Billie remove them, restored the wall and left — again, all without speaking.

One of the bulbs contained water that Billie was glad to see. She sipped in desert fashion, thinking she did not know how long this bulb might need to last. The other two bulbs held food — of a sort. One was a white paste — sweet and soft; the other was mottled green and yellow, a gelatinous starchy compound that was slightly more solid. Neither had any odour she could detect. Billie set the food bulbs up in the recess of the window thinking she wasn't quite that hungry yet.

She stared down the hallway. She stared out the window. She paced. The shadows outside had reached their minimum and started to lengthen when Billie had her next visitors. She was getting tired, and had settled at the end of the concrete bed with her back to the wall, one foot on the floor and the other straight out in front of her. The far door clattered, but Billie didn't move.

Three brown Ultras came to the inside door. She recognized the one with the scar who had brought her clothes in the back; the other two she had not seen before. They were identical. The lead Ultra had a control device similar to that which the gold-skinned, would-be rapist had used. He touched the device and two circles of light appeared on the wall across from Billie. "Put your hands on the circles," he commanded.

Billie stared at the three large figures and felt amused. They're afraid of little old me, she thought and did not move. Part of her could not help but wonder why.

"Put your hands on the circles," repeated the Ultra.

"What are you going to do with me?" demanded Billie.

"That is to be determined by the jurors. Now. Put your hands on the circles."

Billie got up slowly and complied.

"Step back," said the Ultra. Billie took her hands down and stepped back. The Ultra touched a control and her feet froze to the ground.

"Put your hands in the circles again."

This put Billie in an uncomfortable position. She was off balance leaning forward, which seemed to be exactly what the Ultra wanted. Her hands froze to the wall. Only then did the Ultras came into the cell. One of the twins wrapped a scarf-like piece of synthetic material around her wrists, and then her ankles. The bands fused into solid cuffs. He stepped back and nodded to the Ultra with the control panel.

Billie's hands came free from the wall and she pushed herself back to stand upright. The scarf was contracting. Slowly Billie's arms were drawn together and locked in a v-shape in front of her. She could hardly move. Her feet were freed and the scarf around her ankles contracted similarly. She was left able to hobble but not much more.

The Ultra with the scar took her by the arm and led her out of the cell, down the hallway into yet another hall and out of the building. The small city square to which they emerged was paved with interlocking stone blocks.

Billie paused and took a deep breath. The air was cool and humid. The Ultra pulled her arm forward. Still barefoot, she had to walk carefully. In a way it was good that she could hardly move — it gave her time to take a good look around.

An image of the flat and open prairie desert flashed through her mind and she felt a sudden deep pang. Here, everything was rock and roughly hewn. She saw nothing growing, nothing green — just old stone buildings, mountains and sky. The Ultra yanked her arm again, dragging her toward the side of a large building across the square. Billie shuffled along in reluctant baby steps trying to take it all in.

In the side of the building, a small and unobtrusive door opened leading to another hallway. There was writing on the wall in a script Billie did not recognize. Without even thinking about it, she kept track of her directions. They led her through the building to a large, high-ceilinged room, with a vaguely administrative air. She was deposited in a chair beside one of three central tables. On the other side of the room, one table was separate and raised on a low pedestal. Her bare left foot was frozen to the floor and then her arm and leg cuffs were turned back to silk and removed. The scarred Ultra with the control device sat behind her and the other two departed.

Billie sat and looked around with some curiosity. Ultras of various types were sprinkled randomly in chairs about the circumference of the room. She could see males and females; red, green, blue and golden-skinned Ultras with two, four or six arms. Many were apparently identical, twins or clones. The only pattern seemed to be that they almost always stood with others of the same colour and appearance. They all wore the same silvery, open-sided poncho.

The west wall through which she had entered was panelled in a deep-coloured wood she did not recognize. High windows etched the north and east walls of rough, unfinished stone. A large mediaeval-style tapestry with knights and oddly out-of-perspective trees and cities stretched across the bottom of the southern wall.

A blue, two-armed Ultra entered the room and sat beside Billie. He looked at her feet and glanced at the brown Ultra with the panel. "I am to represent your argument," he said, giving the impression of bearing an immense burden.

Billie decided to ignore the Ultra's emotional baggage. "Represent me to whom?" she whispered.

The Ultra seemed surprised she had spoken. "The jurors," he said.

A golden-skinned, six-armed Ultra, who looked identical to her would-be rapist, entered and sat at the table beside theirs on the right. He scowled at Billie for a moment, then busied himself with an electronic pad. A moment later three other Ultras, a blue, a green and a gold, entered and sat at the elevated table. The gold on the left was six-armed; while the blue on the right was four-armed. The green had only two arms, but his head was huge. It was easily twice as big as would have been proportional for the rest of his body. Billie promptly dubbed him the blockhead. The Ultras started talking in their sing-song language.

For some time the discussion went around the room and Billie lost her patience. "Hey. What is . . . " she started.

"Be quiet!" thundered the blockhead.

"I want to know . . . "

"Be quiet!" interrupted the blockhead again. "You will be quiet or you will be restrained. Is that clear?"

After a pause, the Ultras went back to their sing-song deliberations. Billie was stung by the injustice of it. She began to burn with a slow fury. It was manifestly unfair, but there didn't seem to be much she could do about it.

She settled back to watch the undercurrents, the facial expressions and body language — the emotional byplay acted out in front of her, while the Ultras talked in a language she did not understand. There was a lot of simple question and answer. A couple of times there were arguments. The golden scowler liked to walk around and wave all his arms. He paced, he prowled, he tiptoed between the tables as he argued. Her advocate seemed to delight in making pointed comments that derailed the scowler. A lot of the normal conversation was uninterpretable — emotionally neutral.

The afternoon passed in a surreal haze. Most of the Ultras looked bored, but the blockhead kept things moving along. At one point, Billie watched a holographic miniature of herself in the middle of the room. It was recorded while she was frozen to the ground beside the dead gold in the farmyard. A wave of nausea swept her and she quickly looked away. While Billie studied the floor by her frozen foot, she heard the holo of the tall blue asking her questions. The sound stopped and Billie looked up to see the point of view had shifted to an aircar. She saw the farmyard and distant figures, including herself, from the air. This time, it didn't bother her. The fire and figures had an oddly shimmering appearance. Slowly the aircar circled outward in a spiral. The holo winked out. Much heated discussion ensued.

A little later, a video display was activated on the east wall, surprising Billie. It looked like an ordinary stone wall, but it wasn't. The display was large, perhaps six metres square. On the wall played an interrogation Billie did not remember. She was naked, sitting in a kind of bathtub, splashing water and talking a blue streak. As Billie sat and watched the image of herself rambling on about the Machine City, the Dead City, Harmer, whatever passed through her drug-addled mind, a cold feeling of dread swept down her back. She remembered none of this. Her anger and feeling of injustice grew. The wall display was switched off and language was once again denied her.

Billie sat and fumed. The day wore on. Suddenly everything stopped. All the Ultras left except for the scarred one with the device. None of them spoke to her. The two brown Ultras reappeared. She was bound once again and taken back to her cell. The food bulbs were gone from the window where she had left them. A short time later more food bulbs were sphinctered through the wall. Billie was hungry and ate a little of the yellow-green, semisolid gunk. She dozed fitfully; caught herself falling off; dozed again. By the time the light band dimmed, she was stretched full out and sound asleep.

The next day started like the first. The same Ultra brought her breakfast, which again she did not eat. An hour or so later, the trio returned. They shackled her in the same way and took her back to the high-panelled room.

There were not as many Ultras as there had been the day before. Her representative and the scowler were already present. Shortly after she arrived the blue, gold and green trio at the high table walked in and unceremoniously sat.

The blockhead manipulated some control recessed into the table, looked around and said, this time in English, "Are we ready?"

"Wilhemina Featherstone, you are alleged to be responsible for the most serious . . ."

He broke off as a large and skinny, mottled-gold Ultra burst through the main doors waving a pad in one of his six arms and calling out to the trio. He had the most remarkable eyes. They were large, saucer-like and completely black — no white, no iris. Billie was reminded of the extinct primate — the loris. The effect was slightly disconcerting. Otherwise he was tall like all of the Ultras, about two metres, and wore the same open-sided poncho top with loose, full-length utilitarian pants made of the same silvery material. His tawny, spotted, gold colour made him look like he spent a lot of time outdoors. He was sunburnt, Billie decided, unlike the other Ultras who, for all their varied colours, looked like city people who spent most of their time inside.

Everyone stared at the intruder, then for a moment pandemonium reigned as they all tried to talk at once. The blockhead stood and struck the table once with the flat of his hand. The crack echoed loudly and all conversation ceased. He said something placatingly to the group, then looked at the sunburnt intruder and spoke a brief phrase.

The intruder smiled and replied in English, "Gladly."

The black-eyed Ultra approached the display deck and inserted a data crystal. A view of North America as seen from nearby space appeared on the wall. The camera did a series of close-ups; each step bringing more detail. It homed in on the ruins of a large city. She saw kilometres of broken buildings and collapsed debris. With a start, Billie recognized the nuclear blast pattern around the southern side of the Dead City. Still the camera moved in. There were some tiny specks moving along a road. Another two steps and Billie recognized herself and Harmer as they started to follow his trail south from the city. The display froze and the window shrank to a miniature against one side of the screen.

The distant view once again filled the screen, but this time it looked odd. It waved and flowed in false colours. In the corner Billie noticed a spectral curve, labelled in Ultra writing. It was, she guessed, an alternate wavelength image, probably infrared. The sequence played again, this time with shimmering edges and flaring improbable colours. The close-ups stopped, and again the display froze on the aerial view of Billie and Harmer leaving the city. There was something awry with Harmer's temperature. He was flaring beside Billie's glow.

The saucer-eyed Ultra spoke briefly in the sing-song language and with a theatrical wave directed attention back to the wall display. The picture switched to normal vision, remaining in the extreme close-up, and they watched Billie and Harmer walk backwards into the Dead City. Gradually, the shadows grew longer and longer onscreen. The Ultra marked the location on the screen with a graphical tool.

Then the Ultra ran the same sequence backwards in the infra-red wavelengths. Again Harmer flared and Billie glowed. As they moved backwards, the colour of Harmer faded. Finally Billie's glow was brighter than Harmers. And then Harmer disappeared altogether. His temperature had exactly matched the background. The black-eyed gold put the two images up beside each other and made what sounded like a derogatory remark. With a start, Billie realized why they didn't see Harmer at the farm: He could control his skin temperature.

A palpable silence filled the room. The saucer-eyed Ultra broke into a sing-song speech. He turned back to the display deck and the image of Harmer launching the nanocarbon drone appeared. He looked up and the image froze. The display pulled into an extreme close-up of Harmer's face. Then jumped to fill only half the screen. Beside the image, another record appeared. It was an old-fashioned front and side shot of the same face in an old-fashioned military uniform. A brief image of Harmer lying in a fuming enclosure, a cryonic storage unit, made Billie realize he had been in suspended animation.

That was why he had shown up so long after the war. But who would have freed him? Maybe that was why the gold rapist had seemed to recognize Harmer. The saucer-eyed Ultra spoke briefly in their maddeningly incomprehensible language, then shut off the display.

The blue, gold and green judges conferred briefly in whispers. Then the blockhead cleared his throat and spoke. "Wilhemina Featherstone, the arguments against you are unproven. The evidence is circumstantial and a plausible alternative now exists." He glanced at the wall where the display had been. "You are released without prejudice into the recognizance of Arnimalayandagoton."

A stir passed through the room. Ultras stood and milled, some talking loudly. Arnimalayandagoton smiled widely at Billie. The blue, gold and green trio left abruptly. Billie turned and looked at the brown Ultra with the control panel. He stood and angrily slammed the device down on the table beside Billie, then stalked off.

Arnimalayandagoton retrieved his data crystal and walked up to Billie. "Call me Arnim," he said looking at the panel distastefully. Suddenly he noticed the prosecuting gold, who stood scowling at him and Billie. The brown Ultra and several others stood behind him. Arnim lost his smile and seemed to actually shrivel in front of Billie's eyes.

"Come on. Let's get out of here," he said picking up the device. "I can't believe they would actually use a beast lock on you," he muttered to himself, manipulating a control. Billie felt her foot move freely. She flexed her leg and stood up. "Let's go," said Arnim, then leaned over beside Billie's ear and whispered, "Quickly."

Arnim led Billie out the main doors, down into the square outside. Knots of other Ultras stood around and watched them pass. "We'll pick up your stuff and get out of here. Hurry." Arnim was quite anxious. He led the way back to the detention building and into a long, grey room Billie did not recognize. A light band ringed three walls and a console sat at the end by the door. Arnim went to the console and started a search.

"Ah yes. Here it is." He worked a number pad set on the side of the console. On the unlit wall a section flowed open and extended like a filing cabinet. Inside were Billie's shoes, her belt pouch and shoulder bag. All of her nanotools were still there.

She grabbed her boots and started putting them on. Arnim was already at the door. "Come quickly!" he hissed. Billie jumped to follow, fitting her belt as she ran.

"The Eyrie folk are unhappy with us, especially the Argyl clade," he said, leading her out through a door to the east; "Very unhappy." The door led into a narrow alley. They hastened away then turned into a wider road. No one else was about. Another corner and they stepped into a gravelled clearing where several aircars sat.

Arnim led Billie to the third car. They were all the same roughly brick-shaped design with rounded corners and a single window wrapping around the front. He touched a panel on the side behind the window and a portal opened. He stepped quickly inside. For a second Billie wondered if she should run. She could get away from Arnim now. She remembered the golden scowler and decided. She jumped inside.

"Sit down and hang on for a second," said Arnim over his shoulder as he disappeared into a stubby hallway. Billie was in the back of an aircar similar to the one used to carry the buffalo, except this one had a door to the front and no apparent front doors. Arnim was leaning into the cockpit area, his head through the hatchway.

"Dexter 12, Connect flight plan Gamma-3b, emergency take off. Execute."

He returned to the still open portal and peered outside as the craft started to rise. Billie sat huddled on the floor with her back to the wall, holding her shoulder bag. She could see a slice of the ground and then the Ultra enclave, sideways through the doorway. Half a dozen Ultras, including the brown scar-faced one, ran around the corner. Arnim touched a wall panel, and the portal irised shut. Without saying anything, he went back into the front and sat at the pilot's console. For a minute Billie did not move. She could feel tiny jerks and bumps vibrating through the wall and floor as they rose.

Once the craft was airborne and accelerating away, Arnim seemed to undergo a personality transplant. No longer was he running afraid; he suddenly became the jocular idiot. He sat in the pilot's chair smirking back at Billie through the open doorway to where she sat. Billie felt suddenly afraid. She had never spent time around Ultras and she did not really know what to expect. The prospect of spending time cooped up in an aircar with this unpredictable stranger made her uneasy.

"Well you have got yourself in a pretty pickle," he laughed at her.

Billie looked at him blankly.

"Isn't that the way you people like to talk? All that flowery old speech?" He looked momentarily like he had eaten something that disagreed with him.

Billie remained silent, now with a slightly determined jut about her mouth.

"Well, no matter," the Ultra went on as though dismissing the servant of an errant thought. "I suppose you're wondering why I got you out of that dreadful affair. Really the way those anal compulsives do go on!" He waved two arms on his right side.

At this Billie looked up, a smile and the beginnings of interest on her face.

"It was obvious, you know. They find you in a beast lock. The murder weapon was old miltech, which you did not have. It's obvious there had to be someone else around, someone their scanners couldn't detect. But they get so set in their ways. The poor dears. They decided long ago infrared was the thing to use and they didn't change. Well, of course, I had to rescue you."

A look of disbelief ran over Billie's face.

"Well speak up!" commanded Arnim. "What's the matter? Did they damage you?" The Ultra spoke as though he were talking about a piece of machinery.

Billie shook her head.

"So! You are sentient after all. I was beginning to wonder."

One disconcerting aspect of Arnim's eyes was that you couldn't tell where he was looking. His head pointed in her direction, but he might have been looking at the wall above her head, or the floor beneath her . She couldn't tell. Billie found her attention sliding around Arnim's solid black and oversize eyes, somehow never quite focusing, never quite satisfied.

"Well aren't you going to say anything, Wilhemina Featherstone? It's going to be one dull trip." Arnim shook his head in mock exasperation.

"Billie," she said, "Call me Billie."

Arnim turned back from the pilot's console, suddenly all smiles and smarm. "Ah sweet bird of communication! She can talk," he sighed. "Okay. Billie it is. Now aren't you glad I rescued you girl?"

Billie bridled at the "girl," but kept her face neutral. She nodded stiffly.

"Well Billie," Arnim went on, ignoring or missing the emotional subtext, "Today is your lucky day. I am your shining knight. I have rescued you and now I am going to take you home." He paused theatrically, looking at a supremely unimpressed Billie. With an air of magnanimous completeness, he finished, "After a slight detour."

"Detour?" echoed Billie.

Arnim was more interested in monologue than dialogue. "No. The citizens of that wee eyrie are not at all happy with us. I couldn't have left you there. The Argyls would have killed you. Oh nothing official. You would just have had an unfortunate accident." He turned back to the console momentarily.

"It has nothing to do with justice; nothing to do with morality. The poor dears are upset. Funny that a superior should be so much like a sapiens. They're not used to murder, you see. Actually they're not used to anyone dying violently. Ironic really. Considering the world we live in."

It seemed to Billie he could go on talking as long and as wide as he wished and still not say anything useful.

"Come sit up here, where we can talk." He pointed to the copilot's chair beside his. "No. The Argyls were most unpleased!"

Billie was a little startled by Arnim's turn of phrase "the superior." He meant homo superior, a species, not just superior in the sense of better, she realized. It reminded her of the way some males in the village spoke of man or mankind when they meant humanity. Arnim chattered on about superior power struggles, the rivalry between clades, as Billie got up and moved into the front. She saw the land below through the window for the first time. They were high, about two thousand metres in the air heading out into the desert. She sat down, staring out the window.

"Why are your eyes like that?" she asked cautiously.

Arnim seemed to be amused by her question. At any rate he laughed. "An unintended consequence, I am told. You mix and match the genes and characteristics you want, and sometimes they interact in unforeseen ways. The design of new life forms is more of an art than a science."

Billie had to stop herself from staring at him.

"Hang on," said Arnim, "It's about time for us to mysteriously disappear." All at once her heart was in her mouth. Billie looked down. The ground was approaching very fast. She felt queasy and braced herself involuntarily. The craft levelled off about four metres from the ground and swung back northwestward toward the mountains. Billie was glad to see her sense of direction still functioned in these circumstances.

Armin chattered on. "It was a fluke really. I wasn't supposed to be anywhere near the Eyrie, but I had an equipment breakdown. And there you have it. The Argyls and that Argyllevendatanindapuk in particular are such satyrs anyway. If it has a hole, he'll shake his giggle stick at it. I don't know why they keep making that model." Arnim looked at Billie speculatively. "Not that I have anything against taking my pleasures where I find them. But he was useless."

Billie did not know what to make of this suddenly talkative creature. She was not sure if he were referring to Argyl-whatever, the individual or the type of Ultra. "Do all you Ultras have both short and long names?"

"Ultras? Is that what you call us?"

Billie nodded. Suddenly Arnim turned for all the world as if he were delivering a monograph. "Yes, the full genomic model name is too awkward so the universal convention is to use only the first two syllables. The extra syllables are just honorifics anyway." He gazed at Billie with an unreadable expression, then changed emotional directions. "We could just as well have numbers. What do you say? Do you prefer Arnim7 or Arnimalayandagoton? It's all vanity anyway. We could just as easily drop the honorific and half the genomic syllables."

Billie felt out of her depth. Arnim always seemed to bounce from an unexpected angle. She couldn't tell what he was thinking. It made her hesitant. And the thing with his eyes just made it worse. She couldn't tell where he was looking.

"I live back that way," she pointed to the east.

"After a slight detour," said Arnim again, with a cat who ate the canary grin.

"Detour to where?" asked Billie.

"Ah. Now you talk. A sensible woman concerned with directions and goals. I like that." Billie again had the impression he was just warming up and could go on indefinitely. What was it Finian called it? The blarney machine. Arnim definitely had a fully functional blarney machine. "Heaven knows, I tried. As sure as I am vat born, I did not talk down to the wee beastie. I was 'the very model of a modern major general'. I was polite. I saved her life. And to what avail?" He was waving four arms around now as he declaimed. "She has not even asked me why."

Billie sat back and watched the Ultra go on, still not sure just what to think. Outside the craft rose and fell hugging the contour of the land.

"We have to stay under their radar, you see."

Billie did not know what Arnim meant. "What radar?" She looked at him curiously.

"Why from the Eyrie of course. Some of those nasty boyos will be setting out to follow us, of that you can have no doubt."

Billie frowned. She didn't understand. She reverted to her old question. "What detour?"

Arnim seemed to take her questions as a springboard to simply say whatever he felt like saying. "I am Arnimalayandagoton. I am interested in . . ." he paused. "Well, I am interested in everything, but I study old life, dead things — fossils, ruins, the old human records, history, anthropology. I'm a digger." He examined Billie. "Aren't you going to ask me what I am doing here? What you are doing here?

Billie said nothing, but that didn't slow him down in the least. "Just think. The opportunity to investigate an original human in the wild." Arnim turned and looked toward Billie. "You know, I've studied you people, but I've never had the chance to meet one of you before. You really must tell me about the Great Lodge."

Billie looked at him sharply, but still said nothing.

"Are you being quiet because you are afraid?"

The direct question stopped Billie cold. She laughed. "Who me afraid? No. You must be imagining things," she retorted sarcastically. She had seen more Ultras in the last week than in her whole life and that whole drug interrogation business made her skin crawl. It was disgusting. Billie snorted. On the other hand, she did have her throwing knives back again, and she could probably show this golden streak a thing or two if she had to.

Arnim seemed to find her state of mind amusing. "Well landagoshen and by my stars — isn't that the way you people talk?" He didn't wait for an answer. "Here am I, stuck in an aircar with a feral human and she is afraid of me. Now don't that beat all?" He slapped his leg and laughed like he had seen it done in a movie.

Again Billie had the impression it didn't matter much what she said. Arnim seemed to be talking to an invisible audience. He looked intently at Billie. "Why are you afraid?"

Without blinking Billie replied. "I don't know you and you have the power."

Again Arnim did an emotional ninety degree turn and suddenly sounded just like Finian in one of his more correct moments. "Quite right. An accurate appraisal. Well you may know me better before we're through, but the power dynamic I cannot change." Arnim turned back to the pilot's console and started checking screens.

"What detour?" repeated Billie in the sudden silence.

"You're really very beautiful, you know," said Arnim with a curiously distracted air, as though they were sailing down a river on a protracted romantic liaison, "in a miniature sort of way."

Outside they were entering the mountains. The aircar slipped into a pass. Billie started to object. "I live back . . . "

Arnim reached over with his top right arm and squeezed Billie's shoulder. He held the index finger of his top left hand to his mouth, indicating silence. Billie didn't know what to think. Was somebody listening?

"Just a little detour. Let's make it a surprise." Arnim changed gears and blathered on. "Its really very odd you know. If that ground scanner had not gone on the fritz, well I never would have gone near the Eyrie, I never would have seen the broadcast of the trial and I never would have met you," he finished with a flourish. "Isn't that odd?"

Billie decided to sit back and just watch the Ultra, just watch where they flew, just watch everything. Every time she thought she had a handle on Arnim, he did some unexpected thing. It was like he put forward pieces of himself designed to befuddle her. Billie had moved from fear, through hesitation to outright confusion. I should just stop trying to figure him out, she decided. It just hurts my head.

Arnim chattered away, and Billie paid scant attention. She had overloaded on logic and levels and simply didn't want to think.

She looked out the window at a bleak and forbidding landscape. The valleys glinted with black and iridescent nanoslag, none of it moving. Overhead bare mountain rock rose for thousands of metres. Wherever there had been life, there was now only black nano. Billie watched in grim fascination. Valley after valley as they threaded their way to the coast revealed the same. No green. No motion. Nothing living. Even the Machines were dying.

Arnim had fallen silent, and when Billie turned to look at him, he looked afraid. More, he looked terrified. He stared out the window at the dead nano. "Revolting excrescence," he whispered, shivering with dread. Billie watched him pull himself together and busy himself with the console. He was programming something on one of the screens. Billie stared for a while, then her attention drifted back outside. Kilometre after kilometre of the black inertness lay below.

The aircar was moving quickly. When they had crossed the mountains, they turned south and Arnim said "We'll make better time now." The aircar accelerated and the kilometres flew by. Billie watched the rolling waves in fascination. She had never seen the Pacific before.

"I suppose we really should try to save some of the Machines. Before they're all gone," said Arnim presently.

Billie looked up in surprise. "What do you mean?"

Arnim gestured out the window. They were flying over a section of nanoslag that reached right into the ocean. Billie had a glimpse of waves breaking on black iridescence. "That's what the Eyrie folk are doing you know. Reprogramming the nano to kill itself, mechanical apoptosis. A completion virus, they call it. Nasty brutish stuff. Almost as bad as the surge itself." He paused gazing out the window at the swift moving scene below. "Still, it would be good if we could restore some of the people. We may be able to salvage something. What do you think? Did the Old Ones want to live forever in nano or was it all a big mistake?"

"I don't know."

"Ah yes, the sensible woman." said Arnim dismissively, and finally fell silent.

Billie was stiff. She felt cramped and she was hungry. She stretched, arched her back and massaged her legs. Arnim watched in amusement. Billie had the impression he would be amused by any damned thing she did. He did seem to pay an inordinate amount of attention to her. She rummaged in her shoulder bag for the last of her Mission food, pulled out a bit of hardtack and started eating.

"There are energy supplements in the back." Arnim indicated the door. Billie nodded and went on chewing. Outside the ocean was on one side of their craft and the mountains on the other. She finished the biscuit and rummaged again. She pulled out a piece of dried dog meat and started chewing.

Arnim looked at what she was eating. "By the vat! Is that what I think it is?" he exclaimed.

Billie looked at him nonchalantly. "Coyote."

A look of utter revulsion flashed across the Ultra's face. For a second Billie thought he was going to lose it right there. He got up sharply and hustled through the back door. "Carnivores!" he exclaimed. "Bloody primitive carnivores!" he stomped into the rear compartment. Billie sat and unconcernedly finished everything in her shoulder bag. Well that's one way to stop him examining me, she thought.

Outside the landscape stayed much the same. A lane of black nanoslag lay between the mountains and the ocean. It occurred to Billie that she had not seen a recent topographical map of the world. All the data cubes in the village dated from before the fall. How extensively had the machines modified the land, she wondered. How much more had the sea level risen?

Her water bottles were empty and the dried meat made her thirsty. Billie went into the back looking for water. Arnim was lying on a bunk built into the side wall. He opened one eye and watched her. Billie looked around. It was a small space and the bunk had not been there before, which made her wonder. There was nothing obviously holding water.

"Is there any water?" she asked.

Arnim opened both eyes and put his top arms behind his head. He grinned at her as if in some private joke. "Ship. Water dispenser open." A section of wall similar to that at the jail flowed open to reveal a small fountain in the wall. Billie drank and refilled her bottle. When she looked back at Arnim, he appeared to be asleep again and she moved quietly back to the cockpit. As she moved through the doorway, Arnim opened one eye to watch her, but said nothing.

✦

Billie watched the ocean on one side and the mountains on the other drift by. An hour or so later, Arnim came out of the back compartment looking composed and equable once more. He sat in the pilot's chair.

"Are you ready to tell me where we are going yet?" Billie asked.

Arnim favoured her with a tolerant and superior smile. "Of course, my impatient friend. Now that you cannot escape, I can tell you."

Billie looked at him startled. "So?" she prompted.

Arnim continued his irritating smile.

"So where are we going?" demanded Billie.

"Why Antarctica, of course, that's where the only remaining Machines are." Arnim replied with a smug air.

"Antarctica! That will take days," she spluttered.

"Oh no" said Arnim, "this craft is quite fast you know."

Billie sat back considering. The aircar rose to cross a line of peaks which extended into the ocean. They came over the lip of a high valley. A long tarmac was visible. Arnim was busy with the pilot's console, as Billie looked down at the scene below. A cluster of buildings blazing with lights in the daytime sat at one end of the tarmac. As they drew nearer to the buildings, Billie could see several aircars of various designs clumped nearby. One large grey triangular shaped craft stood off to the side. Several colours of Ultra stood on the field.

Billie started to turn to Arnim and again he caught her by the shoulder. Again he signified be silent. Damn sometimes, it's like he has six eyes, not six arms, Billie thought as she turned to look back out the window. The craft slowed and approached the tarmac. They hovered briefly and settled beside the large triangular craft. None of the Ultras on the ground seemed to be paying any attention to them.

Arnim stood and removed a small device from the ceiling between their seats. Billie had not noticed it before. He looked down at Billie. "Come on, let's go. I've always wanted to see this hellhole."

Arnim touched the wall panel in the back and the portal irissed open. A wave of hot air struck Billie as he stepped outside. She picked up her bag and followed slowly. Arnim went to the exterior panel. The wall solidified once again and the aircar rose, heading towards the south.

"One advantage of being a low-level programmer is knowing how things work. I disabled the video recorder and the audio holds only a subset of our conversation. The flight recorder doesn't know we stopped here." He gave her a grin and turned towards the large grey craft.

"I don't know that they are following. Some might be. The taste for public justice is rare in the superior. Usually such matters are dealt with privately." He turned to watch the aircar disappearing in the south.

"That craft belongs to the Eyrie. Sooner or later, they will realize we are not in the desert and they will search by satellite transponder. When they do that, they will find it on Antarctica. Then they will play back the flight path and cockpit recorders and begin to wonder." He continued towards the large grey craft.

He had slipped into his talkative mood again. "The goal is not to lie. The truth is fine right out in the open. It always seems to get out anyway. No. The optimal strategy is to throw in enough red herrings to cause confusion. Make them wonder. That will slow them down just long enough."

Billie shook her head in disbelief. "So where are we going?"

Arnim was suddenly alert. He looked around the field suspiciously. "There are others. Come."

Flight

"Human beings and the natural world are on a collision course. Human activities inflict harsh and often irreversible damage on the environment and on critical resources. If not checked, many of our current practices put at serious risk the future that we wish for human society and the plant and animal kingdoms, and may so alter the living world that it will be unable to sustain life in the manner that we know. Fundamental changes are urgent if we are to avoid the collision our present course will bring about."
— World Scientists' Warning To Humanity (November 18, 1992)

✦

THE TRIANGULAR CRAFT WAS LARGER THAN it appeared from the air. It sat on short telescoping metal legs that flared into a wider pads on the ground. When they got right up to it, Billie saw the metal was a glassy grey material that was new to her. The thought crossed Billie's mind that she would love to take a sample of the metal back to Finian. On the side of the ship, the name Artemis was emblazoned.

Arnim manipulated a control on his belt, and a portal opened on the front side. A short ramp extended. The walls were thick, deep, showing a surprisingly small interior. Arnim looked at Billie and bowed, sweeping the air with three arms and holding the other three out to the side, gesturing for her to enter. He followed right behind. Once they were inside, Arnim touched a wall panel, and both the interior and exterior doors flowed shut.

"Artemis. Identify human present."

A mellifluous, if slightly mechanical, female voice said "Name?"

"Billie Featherstone," said Arnim.

"Status?" enquired the ship.

"Passenger. No command privileges."

"Noted," said the ship.

Arnim looked at Billie. "Come on. I'll show you to your quarters."

"My quarters?"

"Yes. Your room. You may as well be comfortable. You may want to sleep." He started down the cargo hold, skirting various block-like cabinets protruding from the walls, floor and ceiling. In the centre of the back wall, a steel table was fixed incongruously in the air. To one side of the table was a phonebooth-sized block of the glassy metal. Arnim pointed to it and said, "Please read the instructions before trying to use the toilet." Four oval doors marked the end of the hold.

Arnim opened the door on the right and looked back at Billie. "You can put your bag in this compartment."

Billie pushed into the dark room, then looked back at Arnim with a frown. "Compartment?"

"Sorry I forgot." He paused a second. "Artemis, Billie's user level is naive. Restricted spectrum. Language English. Adjust."

"Acknowledged," said the smooth female voice. The lighting in the room brightened and a panel formed on the wall. One section was labelled Open and Billie touched it. The wall did its flowing open trick and Billie put her bag inside. She didn't remove her belt pouch.

Arnim pointed to the lower of two bunks nestled three quarters of the way into the front wall of the room. "There are straps you should use when you sleep." He moved from the door. "Come on. I'll show you the rest."

Arnim strode towards the front. He was quite at home, Billie noticed, picking his way quickly through the messy cargo hold. She took her time following, looking at the cabinets, the odd square blocks and equipment. She poked her head through the hatchway into the front and stopped in surprise. The front of the craft was transparent. She walked wondrously onto the bridge.

"But how? It looked like metal from the outside."

Arnim looked at her in amusement. He was perched in a large central chair in front of a wrap-around console. Enthroned might have been a better word. The chair was ornate, with an organic look. Arches and ridges crossed the back. Extensions with various tools, cables and displays rose from the base. He turned the chair back toward the console.

"It's just a display. You'd better sit down," he nodded sideways to an acceleration couch, which sat along the transparent wall on his left. Through the walls and floor Billie could see that the ship was starting to rise.

Billie sat on the edge of the couch and it moved. She jumped up. Arnim caught the motion in the corner of his eye, and turned to her. "It's smart. It will move as you wish it."

Billie sat on the edge of the couch again, and swung her legs around to the front. She strained to sit up, momentarily pushing back with her legs, then thought better of it and said, "Make a chair."

Her feet lowered and her head rose. The couch molded itself around her body. An armpiece rose beside the wall.

"You can play with that later. Right now we have to talk. No one can eavesdrop here." Arnim spun his chair to face her. Outside the ship was rising over the lip of the valley. Billie looked down and saw they were heading between two mountains toward the sea.

"We're taking a little detour from our detour," laughed Arnim. "I daresay right now, you are probably pretty confused. Are we coming or going?" He gave her a peculiar grin, then took another right angle turn and flipped back into teacher mode. "I've been using this ship for a while now, doing a low earth orbit survey of surface and subsurface structures."

The Artemis slid down over the ocean. Arnim was watching Billie with glee. "Fuel," he said

Billie frowned and said nothing.

"For the impulse you see. We have lots of energy; we just need something to expel at high enough velocity." He slowed down raising his eyebrows hesitantly. "Equal and opposite reaction?" he prompted.

"Yes I'm familiar with Mr. Newton," said Billie scathingly, "but it does make me wonder where . . . "

"Yes, as I said," Arnim continued, gathering speed once again, "you are probably quite confused by now, and I'm sorry for that, but we can talk freely now." Arnim turned to the console for a second, made a couple of adjustments. Billie felt something vibrating through the chair. Through the transparent floor she saw a tube extending into the water from the wing. Another extended on the other side as well. The Artemis rose and fell matching the swell of the waves.

"I need to explain to you what I am doing and why." Arnim was suddenly earnest. "I need to make you understand, but there is a whole context you do not have."

"Yeah well, some basic facts might be a good place to start."

Billie wondered as she looked at Arnim, whether or not she was interpreting his facial expression correctly. Sometimes she thought she knew exactly what he was thinking and feeling; other times his face and his words were out of sync. Was this him or just the way Ultras were? What else did the genetechs change and could a human ever cross that barrier?.

"The thing of it is, I and a few others want to repopulate the species, but there are problems. It's complicated. First off, there are factions, groups among us you know nothing about. There are two sorts, those based on purpose, like the Repops and the Alters, and those based on genetics, like the Argyls and the Arnims. The common emotional imperatives do it, I suppose." Arnim appeared to Billie to be just thinking aloud. "Anyway, some are happy with the world just the way it is — nice and safe and dead. Others want to create a completely new world. Gentech new species. Just keep filling the world with new mutations and see what happens. They, the Alters, call it alterlife. Then again we Repops — that is my group — we Repops want to do much the same, but with the old species. Of course, most of the others are too involved in their own affairs to even notice."

He paused and appeared to be regrouping. "I do not know if you can grasp what it is like for us, so I will just tell you and you will understand what you understand."

For a moment Arnim looked at Billie, like he half-expected her to answer. She said nothing.

"We were designed by humans for human purposes. We are smarter, faster, stronger than humans. We see and hear more and better, and sure as I am vat born, we are weaker as a whole.

There is no social glue among us. We have no families. We are not so much brought up as we survive benign neglect.

"Among humans, the family is integral. It is helped along by innate responses to the helplessness of infants, by the process of identification as you grow and by pair bonding in adults. We do not have any such responses or behaviour. There is no love. We grow up with no parents but a broodmaster who turns us over to educators as soon as we can walk. If we survive the trials, we are set free to make our own way or not. There is no unity, no coherent voice among us. That is why you think we are erratic. By and large, you see the idiosyncratic actions of random individuals. We work together only with great difficulty.

"We pride ourselves in being superior to humans, but we fight over the same things — power, prestige destiny. I was that way too until . . . " Arnim fell silent.

"Until what?"

He shook his head. Arnim seemed to slump in front of Billie's eyes. He continued, "That jury you faced was not a legal body, it is struck to decide scientific questions. It is one of our very few formal organizations and at that, it is patterned on the old human model of science. You were no more than a psychohistorical detail to them. Your disposition was a matter of supreme indifference, for all but the clones of Argyl." Arnim broke off staring into the distance, then he whispered, "You will always have to watch out for the Argyls."

Billie was finding it hard to pay attention to Arnim's confessions, because they had risen so high that she could now see the curvature of the Earth through the floor. "Why are you telling me this now?" she asked.

"Because you need to know the problems. The Alters have started to hunt us Repops. If you cannot disprove or discount

an idea, kill its advocates. Simple and efficient. Human, even."
He grimaced sardonically.

"Of course that's the interesting thing about the evolution
of ideas," Arnim took another right angle turn to the professorial mode, "the rules always change. There is always another
framework, another context in which to evaluate any given
proposition." Arnim shook his head in resignation and turned
his big eyes to Billie.

Billie stared not knowing quite what to think either of Arnim
or what he was saying.

He didn't give her a chance to react."Anyway, we Repops are
trying to restore the biosphere, or at least shorten the recovery
time. There are not many of us, and it is dangerous now that
we are hunted. There is so much to do and those execrable
Machines are everywhere."

Arnim shivered and steeled himself. "For a while some
thought we might be able to restore the people in the Machine,
but that has pretty much ended. Some faction has begun sowing
a completion virus among the Machines, so it's over for them.
That's why I mentioned the Machines in Antarctica. That bit
of misdirection will really get the Alters going. And lead them
away from us." He chuckled and paused. "Anyway, those people
in the Machine are lost."

Billie looked at him. "I met one of them. Well, I'm not sure
that 'person' is the right word. He was strange, half-human,
half-robot."

"I know," said Arnim with a grin. "That's why we're here."

Billie frowned, as Arnim continued. "I told you we want
to repopulate the species. But there are basic problems. Our
samples are not complete. Our records are not complete. We
have only a couple thousand genomes out of the millions we
need. The old humans set up a genebank, called Vishnu." Arnim

paused. "They knew the extinction was happening, and they couldn't stop it, so they did what they could — they saved the genes." A wave of painful uncertainty crossed Arnim's face. He shut his eyes for a moment. "Or so the records say. We don't have the genes. That is the basic problem. Where are the genes? We can't restore an entire biosphere without the genetic data." He chuckled incongruously.

Billie said nothing. She was looking down through the floor as they rose ever higher.

"And it's all because of you," Arnim announced. He looked at Billie with a twinkle. He inserted a data crystal into a port in one of his chair's accessory tables. "You made this possible. You made this necessary. Just think. If you were an old human and you wanted to stash a few million frozen genes somewhere safe, where would you put them? Anywhere on earth would be vulnerable. There are too many people buzzing around in orbit or at the Lagrange points. Venus is not in the picture. Mars has too many people. The earth side of the moon is similarly out. I thought it would likely be one of the asteroids. It would be far enough away, it couldn't be easily disturbed, and it would be easy to get lost among all those rocks. I spent years researching old rocket flights, old gene bank records, trying to figure out where they might have put it. It never occurred to me they might have done something sneaky until I heard your interrogation."

A section of the front wall began to show Billie's interrogation. She was sitting naked in the water, gaily splashing and talking about the Machine City, black nano, a handful of sand, TFM dissolving. On the wall display, Billie said "the last thing he said was 'Vishnu is in Tsiolkovsky.'"

Arnim shut off the display. For a second it looked like smooth grey metal then it seemed to become transparent again. The sky was getting dark Billie noticed. "You hear that?" said Arnim. "Vishnu is in Tsiolkovsky."

"Yeah. So what the hell is Tsiolkovsky?"

"What! You mean you don't know?"

"No. What is it?"

"Arnim laughed. "Well I'll be damned. She answers one of our burning questions and doesn't even know what it means."

"Yeah," said Billie sarcastically. "It's a knack I've got. I was born old. So what is it?"

"A crater."

"A crater?" Billie echoed

Arnim looked at her. "Artemis, adapt human chair to acceler-ation." He turned back to his console. "You should hang on. This is a bit of a kick."

The tables, tools and cables around Arnim's large chair started retracting and folding into the base. He turned back to the console. Billie's chair also began to move, slowly becoming spongy and rising around her limbs and torso.

"Where is this crater?" Billie asked.

"On the far side of the moon," called Arnim.

A loud roar filled the cabin and the ship bucked. Billie was pushed back into the sponge. She could feel the chair moving, adapting to her shape and structure. Ridges rose along the outline of her body, three-quarters enclosing her. "The moon!" yelled Billie, but her yell was lost in the rocket's roar. Arnim did not answer.

The pressure lasted longer than was interesting. Abruptly, the sound cut down to a distant rumble. Billie gasped. The earth hung below her feet, blue and white and beautiful. Her heart was in her throat and then her last meal was. She quickly swallowed trying to force the acrid taste down. There was no down! She took a deep breath.

Arnim looked at her struggling for composure. "I'll keep a slight acceleration and later deceleration on, but you will still be essentially weightless and may feel queasy. If you're lucky it will pass quickly." He touched his console, and the transparency faded. A pair of normal looking windows appeared at the front of the cockpit.

"I would rather see," said Billie.

"The console will not work for you, but you can use safe verbal commands." He spun his chair around and looked at Billie. "Artemis, transparent mode."

Billie looked around approvingly as the view changed. "Okay so there might be a genebank on the moon. Fine, why am I here?"

Arnim nodded. "There are a complex of reasons. The most basic I suppose is that you humans are involved. It's your world too and you should know we are trying to change it. Our work will affect you sooner or later."

Billie sat back, thinking of the buffalo. She crossed her arms and stared at Arnim appraisingly. The stray thought crossed her mind that even though she was comfortable with this Ultra, she didn't really trust him. "Unh huh. Go on," she said.

Arnim gave her a funny little Ultra smile, like he knew exactly what she was thinking. His face turned suddenly serious. "I could not leave you there. There was some truth to what I said earlier about the Argyls killing you."

Billie did not move. She was becoming more and more skeptical. The story was always changing with him. She stared with her arms crossed, and repeated "Unh huh."

"And finally, a personal foible." Arnim stopped and swallowed. "I don't quite know how to say this. I don't want to be alone," he blurted out. "It's such a perfect opportunity. A week alone in a tin can with a feral human. Can you imagine? How better to learn? I want to know how you think and feel. I want to know how it feels to be you."

Billie snorted in disgust. "You've kept me going, kept me confused, never gave me time to think. I never had any choice. There is this little thing about trust and mutual respect, you know."

Arnim looked like he had been struck. "You're right," he said, "I'm sorry." The apology hung in the air and Billie did not acknowledge it. She felt there was still something else going on. She didn't know what it was and it made her angry.

"Chair. Release," Arnim said and the surface which was molded about his legs and torso flattened. He drifted loose, then pushed himself up in the air. He turned and looked at Billie. "If you don't mind, I'd like to be alone for a while." He pushed himself towards the hatchway and disappeared into the back.

Billie was fit to be tied. What the hell was with this Ultra? "He doesn't want to be alone; then he wants to be alone," she exclaimed "Aaarrh!" As soon as she spoke, she remembered Finian talking about the tragedy of contradictory desires. What had he been talking about? The Old Ones? What? Billie sat and stared at the earth, pondering Arnim's behaviour. She could not encompass his state of mind, his way of being. He seemed to always come out of the blue. Maybe that was a human - Ultra thing. Maybe there was something else to it. He did save my butt, she conceded grudgingly. She slowly calmed down, watching the Earth revolve below.

Australia drifted below, then while crossing Africa, the ship spoke over the intercom. "Attention. Prepare for lunar trajectory burn in five minutes." A minute later Arnim floated back into the bridge. He did not speak, but only nodded to Billie. He floated into position. "Chair. Acceleration mode." The chair started to move and adapt to his form once again.

"There's something you're not telling me." said Billie.

Arnim looked at her. "There are many things I am not telling you. I wonder which it is you need to hear."

Billie felt deflated. She stared at Arnim and did not have a clue what he was feeling.

The rocket kicked in and the pressure rose. Billie struggled to breath smoothly. It felt like someone was lying on top of her. The roar and vibration did not seem to last quite as long this time. Abruptly there was silence. The moon hung directly in front of the craft now.

"Chair. Release," said Arnim and floated loose once more. "Now if you don't mind. I really do need to sleep." He pushed himself from the cabin and Billie was once again alone.

"Chair. Release," she said. For a few minutes Billie floated gazing at the moon. Then she pushed herself to the rear hatchway. Arnim was out of sight and she was far from sleepy. She had been awake for more than eighteen hours, but she was wired by anxiety and strangeness. She started to play with freefall. With the very slight acceleration Arnim had mentioned, an object released in the air slowly drifted towards the back wall, which was now somehow the floor. The arrangement of the craft made more sense once she made that shift. She drifted toward the floor. The toilet had moved itself to stand on the rear wall she noticed with some surprise.

Billie stood on the steel table and launched herself straight up towards the cockpit. She flew the length of the hold, bounced and ricocheted toward one side where a fortuitous ring was embedded in the wall. The rings were strategically placed around and down the cargo hold, she noticed. They might have been intended to tie down cargo, but they also served admirably as handholds. She bounced from one side of the hold to the other, exploring and getting used to the feeling of weightlessness. This was fun!

Back on the table, she launched herself spinning this time. Because of the spin her direction was off and she crashed back first into a wall. Grabbing a ring she launched herself back at the table. Pausing for a second to let a slight vertigo fade, she clung to the top of the table in a crouch. She rose and launched herself straight down the centre of the hold spinning all the way. With a feeling of triumph she bounce-landed by the bridge door and caught a handhold.

Can I spin in a star shape? she wondered. The cargo hold was a little too wide to be able to do it from the side. She could spin, but she always seemed to push herself out away from one wall into another. Perhaps if I jump with a slow spin, I can bend and move into a sideways star. She spent the next hour trying to perfect the manoeuvre. At length, she was played out and retreated to her room to sleep. Her last thought as she fell off was of Arnim and his big-eyed, unreadable face.

Billie did not sleep well. She kept floating away. The lights wouldn't go off. The room smelled like burnt plastic. There were little noises all the time. At one point she woke up on the floor and launched herself back into the bunk.

"I told you to use the anchor straps." said Arnim unsympathetically when she complained the next morning. They sat across from each other at the steel table in the hold, drinking a hot fluid Arnim called syncaf from heated, pot-like containers with a syringe pump in the base. You pressed the bottom plunger and hot fluid squirted through the mouthpiece. The syncaf had a slightly acrid taste that Billie decided she liked.

Arnim finished his breakfast and launched himself toward the bridge. "You should come and see this," he called back over his shoulder. "We turned while you were sleeping and there is a whole new view."

Billie stood and launched herself after him. Arnim hung on the hatchway momentarily watching Billie fly toward him. He pushed into the front. When Billie entered, he said "Artemis. Transparent mode." The front of the chamber cleared. Earth floated in front of them.

"It looks so small. So fragile," said Billie.

"Yeah well she's a tough old gal. Don't let her fool you."

"Can we see the moon too?" asked Billie.

"Artemis. Bubble mode," said Arnim.

Suddenly it was like the ship disappeared. All of the walls, the floor and ceiling of the bridge projected a realtime image from outside. Billie and Arnim floated side by side through space toward the moon. For a second Billie felt like she was falling. She closed her eyes to let it pass. She looked again and suddenly she was flying. The earth. The moon. The sun was a soft hazy circle. Billie soared in rapt wonder. She knew it was magic — a blessing and a wonder she would never forget. The earth was a tiny blue ball in space. She thought of Hannah. "We have not destroyed the garden, Hannah. Not quite."

The moon behind them was noticeably larger now. Billie could see more clearly than ever before, the flat and fused grey surface. Rings of nuclear destruction overlapped and covered the lit portion of the hemisphere. In the unlit portion, Billie could dimly make out a similar lunarscape.

"Where is Tsiolkovsky?" she asked. Arnim spun his chair around and touched a panel sprouting from the side. A slowly revolving holo globe of the moon appeared in the air between them. A blue green flight path lit up indicating an orbit. Billie recognized the hemisphere behind her. The other side was pock-marked with many craters, with only the odd blast site.

"Artemis. Mark Tsiolkovsky," commanded Arnim and one medium-sized crater just below the equator was outlined in red.

"I must admit I do not know much about the far side of the moon." said Billie. "Why was it not flattened too?"

"There were very few people or facilities on the far side — a couple observatories, a couple monasteries. Most people wanted to be able to see the earth, to communicate if not for psychological reasons."

Billie looked at the holo globe. "Do you really think the genes are there?"

Arnim shut off the holo. "I don't know. It's worth checking out." He launched himself through the moon toward the hold. As he approached, the hatch flowed open automatically, and Billie had the peculiar view of a door in space. The cargo hold appeared to stretch toward and into the moon.

"Artemis. Window mode." said Billie. She floated alone watching the earth recede.

✦

As the Artemis swung around the back side of the moon, a short burn put them into lunar orbit. Arnim and Billie floated in the bridge watching the surface below. The holo globe hung in the air in front and to the side of Billie, highlighting the positions of the Tsiolkovsky crater and the ship. The sun disappeared. A series of further minute burns jarred Billie as they passed again into sunlight. The ship was slowing, dropping in a long arc.

Billie sat and stared at the glassy smooth surface. It had always looked that way as long as she remembered, but she had seen the pictures. She had grown up with the stories of the Day with Two Suns. Ah my silver sister, she thought, what we have done to you?

"Artemis. Holo off. Outline Tsiolkovsky on the main display." Arnim remained focused on his console. The front wall was covered with a realtime image of the moon below.

Tsiolkovsky slid below the ship and they appeared to hover. No war damage or buildings were visible. It looked entirely pristine. Desperation was frozen on Arnim's face.

"Artemis. Wide spectrum scan ultraviolet to radio wavelengths, focused on the crater." A background hiss of radio noise became barely audible and the display started showing alternate wavelength views of the surface.

"There is an anomalous radio source four hundred kilometres to port, but I am filtering it," stated the ship.

"That's odd," said Arnim. "I wonder what that is? We'll take a look later. Meanwhile we focus on the crater." He was starting to act fidgety. The Artemis circled the crater once at high altitude.

They studied the display. Billie had the impression Arnim was ready to give up. "Maybe it's underground, somewhere under the rim," she suggested thinking of the disembodied voice back home.

The suggestion seemed to break Arnim out of his despondent mood. "Perhaps," he said, "We can look anyway." They dropped down and circled the crater rim again seeing nothing. Billie had never seen the Ultra look so miserable.

"We'll try one more thing," said Arnim desperately. "Artemis. Run crater video data through an image processing filter - sharp mask and edge enhance. Look for any artificial structure." He guided the ship into another circling of the crater.

They were about a third of the way around, when Artemis spoke. "Artificially straight line detected." An outlining circle appeared on the main display. Billie could not see anything. Arnim turned to his console and the ship glided slowly toward the indicated spot. As they drew closer, a flat semicircle in front of part of a door came into view. It was only visible on an angle.

Arnim looked at Billie with a big grin. "Well done, little one. I was so afraid it was a dead end. Now we get to explore!" He bounded up in glee and bounced off the ceiling. "Oh, first I have to show you the suits. Oh, and before that, we have to land." Billie watched in amusement as Arnim spun, literally and figuratively.

All at once, Arnim grabbed a hold of himself, becoming matter of fact. He sat down again and carefully guided the ship to a landing beside the entrance. "Come on. I'll get you a suit." He bounced back to the cargo hold.

◆

Suddenly it all came to a head for Billie. She was no longer a passenger. The voices of Hannah and Finian, a whole crowd of the People were urging her on. The memory of her dream hovered like an itch just out of reach. The tide had turned in a psychic battle of which she had been only dimly aware. She would help this Ultra, for the People.

"Chair. Release." She turned sideways on her seat and moved slowly to the door. The light lunar gravity was tricky. It would take some getting used to.

Arnim had his head in a cabinet halfway down the hold, pulling out odd items, searching for something. "Ah good. Here it is. I thought there was a small one. Here try it on." He was still bouncing like a hyperactive child.

"Arnim, will you calm down. Please." He handed her a belt with a block of the glassy metal affixed to the middle.

"Yes, of course I will. It's just that I've dreamt of Vishnu all my life. Here put this on. I want to see the look on your face."

The belt was heavy, made of miltech synthetic. It looked like it would hold a good weight - on earth. The small block attached to it was surprisingly dense, weighing about twenty kilograms — on the moon.

Billie took the belt and started to put it on. The weight of the block fooled her and she let one end drop. She reached behind her back trying to grab the free end.

"Wait. I'll get it for you," said Arnim, taking the block in one set of hands while reaching for the free end with another. He held the belt half around her. Billie was suddenly intensely aware Arnim was almost hugging her. She did not want to arouse this Ultra.

Taking the free end and pulling it through the loop, Billie stepped away from him and turned. Arnim was still in a little-boy-bursting-with-fun mood and did not even notice her anxiety.

"This model is for a two-armed teenager and so it should fit you about right. Here, take these bands and put them on your wrists." He handed her two elongated panels with clasps which slipped snugly onto her forearms.

"Okay now what?" Billie asked.

"Turn it on, of course!" He laughed. She looked at one wrist then the other. The panels were identical, just different handedness.

"Redundant. In case . . . " Arnim started to say and she pressed <on>. For a second nothing happened, then she noticed the belt was loosening. No it wasn't loosening. The weight was gone. A motion by her foot caught her eye. Looking down she saw flowmetal forming about her legs. She was covered from the knees down and it was rising. She bent her knees. The metal flexed with ease.

" . . . of damage," Arnim finished his interrupted train of thought, all the while watching her intently.

"Lift your other foot off the floor, too," he said. Billie was covered up to the waist, and before she could blink, up to the neck. The flowmetal moved down her arms integrating with the control panels. It felt like an elastic shirt. Her hands and head were left uncovered.

"What no helmet?" she said to Arnim, holding up a bare hand.

He chuckled. "The flowsuit is fairly smart. It knows you are in an atmosphere. There is a helmet tab there. He pointed at her right control panel. You should spend some time looking at that. It's programmable. See where everything is. It will monitor your heart and breathing and so on. You can trust the suit to do the right thing, almost always."

She gave it a cursory glance. "Yeah? Can I take a pee?"

"Only if you want wet feet."

"Well in that case," Billie said pressing the <off> button, "I want to pee in real gravity." The suit flowed away from the panels, up her arms. A split ran down the front, then down each leg. The flowmetal coalesced in a runnel on her back and then along the back of each leg, finally rising to the block on the belt. "I'm funny that way. I always like to know how to turn a machine off." She bounce-walked in the partial gravity back to the phone booth toilet.

"You did better than I expected," said Arnim to her back.

She spun about and gave him a grin. The toilet definitely worked easier in gravity. When she rejoined Arnim, he was suited, with his head and hands free. Somehow his six arms looked even stranger in the suit.

"Shall we go?"

"Just a sec." Arnim continued digging through the cabinet.

Billie turned her suit on and let it flow. When she was covered as before, she looked at the control panel. There was a hand and an associated number dial display which read <1>. She pressed the <hand> button and gloves formed over her hands. They were light and flexible to her fingers. Pressing the number <7> on the left-arm panel, the glove of that hand thickened and stiffened, becoming a mitten. Beyond the tips of her fingers, a kind of vise grips formed. They opened and closed as she moved her thumb. The force of the grip was amplified by the suit. A pressure display on the panel changed as she pressed her thumb against her fingers.

When Billie pressed <8> on the hand dial, the vise grips became a long thin pry bar. She looked at Arnim in amusement as he turned from the cabinet holding a case.

"Those are just the ten which happen to be currently programmed," he said, placing the case on a convenient flowmetal block. "Press helmet and you'll see the full menu." He lifted the lid. "Ah Good. Just what we need."

He caught Billie's quizzical look and said, "It's a portable sequencer and duplicator. If the genes are here, I'll make a quick copy of some."

She nodded and pressed <1> again. The pry bar flowed back into the suit. She touched <helmet> and felt the metal moving on her neck, by her ears, touching her hair. For a fraction of a second she was in complete darkness. An oddly familiar, burnt sandy smell permeated the suit, then the front of the helmet became transparent. It was the same kind of display the bridge used. Projected over the objects in the room was a series of interactive displays and graphical menus. She looked at the menu labelled BioStatus and it grew in size. The suit was tracking what she looked at — the movement and focus of her eyes. She moved her eyes to an icon labelled Environment and a series of time-sequenced charts labelled atmosphere, gravity and temperature opened.

Billie looked at Arnim. Immediately the Environment display faded and a display opened around him showing suit ID, status, and various biosigns. When she looked at one of the enigmatic blocks of flowmetal on the floor, a label over it read, "Medconsole, currently inactive."

"This is going to be distracting," said Billie. "Can I turn it down?"

"Sure. Just change the verbosity setting."

As Billie adjusted the level, Arnim touched his control panel. Her eyes were drawn to his suit enveloping his head. From the outside it looked like solid flowmetal for a second, then the front cleared and his face appeared. He was laughing.

"Can you hear me?" His voice was via radio in her ear.

"Yes. What's so funny?"

"You looked so concerned. Don't worry. The suits are good. They'll protect you. See your arm."

She looked down to see a solid green band on the end of each panel.

"If you look at Suit Status, you can see the details, but don't worry about it. The suit will do the right thing."

Billie remembered Finian at his skeptical best. "Well, those would be fine and ironic famous last words."

He grinned. "Let's go!" They bounce-walked to the portal and Arnim opened the inner half. "Artemis," he said on the radio, "lunar EVA; probable duration two hours; maximum duration four hours. Monitor."

"Acknowledged," said the ship.

The airlock cycled and they stepped out onto the surface. Billie was not ready for how clear everything looked. The stark grey under brilliant sunlight, etched by utter blackness, captivated her eyes. She turned slowly, stunned by the beauty, the magnificent desolation. When she looked at the sun, the same soft hazy circle as was displayed on the bridge appeared. It was a gentle reminder that everything she saw was mediated via sensors and a smart suit. She kicked the ground and the powdery dust flew surprisingly far. The moon was wrenchingly beautiful. At the same time, part of her quailed. It was utterly devoid of life. The empty lifelessness was a palpable presence.

"It's over here," said Arnim matter-of-factly.

How can he possibly be so blasé about this, she wondered.

An overhang hid the door. A metallic semicircle projecting from the base of the recessed airlock was the only visible sign. The door was open a crack. Arnim pulled the door wide and bowed like a courtly dandy, gesturing for her to enter.

The interior was dark; the door old stainless steel. There was no flowmetal here.

"Suit menu lights," said Arnim behind her. Billie found the control with her eyes and slowly increased the brightness of her helmet lights.

The entrance was more like a cave. The walls and floor were chiselled rock. It led perhaps ten metres to another door, this one closed. On the door, in large bold letters was the name Vishnu Project. On the side of the doorframe someone had scribbled in yellow chalk "speke frende & nter." Arnim turned a mechanical latch with a spoked wheel. Billie did not hear or see anything, but she noticed a blip on the environmental display when he opened the door.

"Carbon dioxide and mostly nitrogen," Arnim said. Hearing nothing but the sound of your own breathing and the occasional radio message was funny-unnerving.

Again he held the door open for her. The second time Billie thought that it was not for manners that he bid her go ahead.

The interior was white, which increased the light level. The walls were smoothly finished — a tube that stretched in front of her and out of sight around a curve.

Arnim propped the door open with a small tube extruded from his suit. Billie started ahead. About halfway down the hall, it widened and a section of wall with a different colour showed where once a larger diameter tunnel had joined. A utility entrance, she surmised.

A stainless steel pressure door reflected suit lights from ahead. It was larger, with the same star wheel locking mechanism. When Arnim spun the latch and yanked, the door barely moved.

"Give me a hand with this," he said. It was stiff and moved slowly because of something other than weight. Billie could feel grinding in the hinges as it slowly opened.

Again Arnim extruded a flowmetal tube to ensure the door did not close. And again Billie found herself in the lead. This was definitely not a coincidence. He was hanging back out of fear. She didn't care.

When she stepped inside, overhead lights snapped on. It was a huge warehouse. An open area, perhaps five metres wide lay directly in front of her. Beyond that, rows of unpainted metal cabinets stretched perhaps a kilometre back. Stacked three high, the meter wide by half meter high cabinets rested on metal racks with pipes and wires leading down from an overhead trelliswork. The rows extended all the way across the half-kilometre width of the room. "Holy shit! It's huge."

"It has to be for over ten million species," said Arnim. She could hear the excitement in his voice, the beginnings of self satisfaction. He moved to a cabinet immediately in front.

"There should be some sort of command-and-control centre around here somewhere. Why don't you take a look for it?" Arnim suggested. He bent over to examine the cabinet.

Billie wandered down the open area feeling distinctly dismissed. She could see nothing looking like a computer console, but set into the wall a couple of hundred metres from the entrance, was a doorway. She bounced in that direction. A large object blocked the way just inside the door. When she turned on her suit lights again, she saw it was an old square industrial robot on wheels. Past the machine, she could see a workroom, a row of consoles and various other lab equipment.

The robot was inert and effectively blocked the entrance. As she struggled to move it, she heard Arnim exclaim, "Oh no," with a strangled sob. Hurriedly she retraced her steps and found him slumped down on the floor. A random half-dozen cabinets around him in the aisle were open. Inside each, were four shelves, with piping but nothing else. Arnim had his eyes closed and all of his arms wrapped around himself swaying slowly from side to side like a baby in a cradle.

"Hey. I need help," said Billie.

Arnim opened his eyes. "What?"

"Come and help me. I found a computer room, but the door is blocked." She held out her hand, which he took to stand. In the back of her mind, Hannah's voice whispered, "focus on the immediate."

The old robot had turned sideways and jammed itself. Moving it without much traction was not easy. The trouble was turning the front gang of wheels. Once they managed that, the robot rolled out of the way easily enough.

The room remained dark, when Billie stepped inside. She noticed with some amusement, that Arnim stayed safely outside. At least part of his behaviour was becoming predictable.

Stepping out of the room, Billie said, "Why don't you check more cabinets. Perhaps they didn't need the ones at this end."

She looked demonstratively around the warehouse. Even in low gravity, it would take some time to walk around the room.

All of a sudden Arnim wasn't sure what was going on and looked at her querulously. "I don't think so," he said, "but I will check." He headed back to the cabinets.

Billie re-entered the computer room, looking for a switch or some manual light control, but didn't see one. The light from her suit reflected from console screens and bottles. A device that looked like a centrifuge was plugged into a bar that ran across the back of a workbench. She examined the tangle of wires and cables dangling at the back. The line from the power bar reached upward. She traced the cables. Optical cables went one way, power another, and a mass of cables she did not recognize went in a third direction. She followed the power cables to a tall row of panels along the back wall and started flipping switches. A faint vibration shook the floor as some remote device activated.

"Did you do something?" Arnim asked over the radio.

"Yeah. I'm looking for a light switch," Billie replied.

He grunted, but said nothing else.

At least he is still functioning, she thought and threw another rocker switch. Along the workbenches lights flickered on. It was not the overhead lights she had wanted, but it was sufficient.

"I'm going to check random cabinets further away," said Arnim.

"Okay. Keep in touch."

In the back of the lab were rooms. Billie stuck her head in one and overhead lights came on showing a meeting room with a large table. Another was a kitchen area. Somebody had lived here, but who? She drifted through the quarters like a ghost. Nothing of consequence remained in any of the rooms. These people had not moved out in a hurry.

Back in the lab, the consoles were all dead. Perhaps they can tell us something, she thought. At the power panels, she threw the remaining switches. On the last one, overhead lights shone and the computers started booting. Billie walked along the consoles looking at the screens. She had never seen systems like these. They were old. Really old.

One station showed:

"%quartz:\root>"

and nothing else. Others lit up, but only with a dim solid light — no characters or graphics.

Another station showed:

"transmitting . . ."

"done"

"transmitting . . ."

"done"

"transmitting . . ."

"done"

scrolling up off the top of the screen. She didn't know how to use these old-fashioned systems.

By a console, near the end of the row, on a pad of paper was written the word, "Iapetus." When she picked up the pad, the paper started flaking. Searching through her suit menu, she found <pockets> and put the fragments of paper in the pouch formed. Then she shut off all the power and went to find Arnim.

Billie followed a trail of open, empty cabinets across the room. Arnim was at the far end, kitty-corner from the computer room and he was in a state. It was pretty clear there was nothing left in the genebank. Arnim was dodging from aisle to aisle going part way down a segment, opening a random cabinet, moving to the crossway, going to the next aisle and zagging back to open another cabinet. She caught sight of him and moved straight along the crossway to catch up to him. Standing at the end of an aisle segment, she watched him open two more empty cabinets.

"Hi Billie," said Arnim in a voice that sounded completely unconcerned — completely detached. He walked right by her. He was just a good dutiful worker doing his job without thinking. The "without thinking" part was what he needed just then she realized.

Arnim reached the last row on the side, and Billie decided to intervene. They had been away from Artemis for over two hours. Arnim turned to start on the next segment heading back across the room and she blocked his path.

"Hey Arnim!" He started to walk past her and she moved in front of him again. "Hey Arnim," she repeated. His eyes were half-closed and he looked like he was about to laugh and to cry at the same time. "We need to get back to the Artemis, Arnim," she said very gently.

He was like a child. "Yes, Billie. Okay. If you think so."

Somehow that behaviour was more unsettling to Billie than violent disagreement would have been. She took him by an arm and they walked back to the big door. At the door she picked up the flowmetal tube and he absorbed it back into his suit without comment.

As soon as they stepped back into the tunnel, the lights in the big room shut off and a sudden wave of fear swept over Billie. She activated her helmet lights. She was deathly afraid of being trapped. Struggling with herself to remain calm, she supported Arnim down the tunnel.

The next door had swung open, and the flowmetal tube had fallen to the rock floor. Billie handed it to Arnim, who seemed to have no inclination to do anything for himself. Again, she took him by an arm and led him. She hadn't noticed Arnim had left a rock in the outside doorjamb. Billie pushed it open.

It is not easy to lead somebody in low gravity, and when they stepped out onto the surface once again, it was more so. The temptation is to take longer bounce steps and somehow they never quite coordinated.

Looking back at the door to Vishnu, Billie noticed a tower with a small antenna had risen above the rocky crater wall. She wondered briefly, if that was the rumble she had felt, but she was occupied guiding Arnim. After a gruelling waltz, they made it back to the Artemis. As she stood in the airlock waiting for the air to cycle, it occurred to Billie that this time she had not even noticed how the surface looked.

With a desperate and despondent air, Arnim re-entered the ship. He was distraught beyond any consolation. Billie had to tell him to turn his suit off. When she turned her own suit off, the paper that had been in the pocket fell to the floor. She picked up the pieces and set them on one of the blocks of flowmetal. Arnim did not protest when she led him like a child and made him lie down. Billie could not cope with his blank haunted stare, and she left him alone, telling him to sleep.

Hungry, she dialed several nutritional supplements and some syncaf, then went to the bridge to eat. The wall display was off. The console had one active screen. She leaned over to look at it. "Microwave data stream received," it said. In the background was a lunar map with a blinking light near the terminator. Their current position in Tsiolkovsky was marked with a small green circle.

"Artemis. Bubble mode." The lunar landscape appeared all around her. She sat and stared at the rocks and powdery sand. Something had changed. It wasn't fun anymore. She wanted to go home. The antenna and tower above the empty genebank rose a good forty metres over the Artemis.

Billie ate her meal slowly and turned her thoughts to Arnim. He was almost nonfunctional. She had to hope he would snap out of it, because she couldn't fly the ship. The Ultra food supplements were not tasting any better with time. Billie drank the syncaf and sighed. Perhaps she should sleep as well, she thought, that way they would be awake at the same time anyway.

Back in her room, she stared at the ceiling a long time, before drifting off.

The Silver Egg

The StarSeed Project
"*Driven by the failure of radio and optical SETI programmes over the previous millennium, and caught by the impracticality of utilizing Planck scale energies for interstellar travel, a consortium of concerned business interests started searching in 2744 for practical methods of extending their domains through interstellar space. The StarSeed Project was designed to accelerate nanobot assemblers to a significant fraction of the speed of light, targeting every star system within a thousand light years. When trigger conditions were satisfied, the assemblers activate, creating the artificial wombs and germ cells required for homo superior replication.*"
— Encyclopedia Solaris [2882 OT Edition]

✦

IT WAS NOT RESTFUL, and it was a long time coming, but finally Billie passed beyond a light half-sleep. She did not hear Arnim get up, but his first call brought her to full awareness.

"Billie! Where are you?" The door to her room irissed open when she was halfway across the room.

"What's wrong?"

"Wrong? Nothings wrong. Come and see. You won't believe it!" The hyperactive child was back. A very happy hyperactive child. "You must tell me exactly what you did in that computer room." He bounced into the room.

Billie pulled back from the Ultra's infectious smile, holding her shirt like a shield. "Okay. Look. I'll tell you ev-ery-thing," she lilted. They locked eyes for a second. "But first, I'm going to get dressed and wash my face. I really need something to drink and my mouth tastes like something died. So If we're not in immediate danger." She pushed Arnim lightly on the chest.

He laughed. He was already heading back toward the bridge. "You won't believe this. It's great!" he bubbled and was gone.

Billie cleaned herself and made a syringe pot full of Arnim's syncaf. She took a big drink and sighed. Well, I suppose it's better than having to mother him, but this could get old fast.

Arnim was hunched over the console. "Just doing a backup to holo crystal," he explained. "Here. This one is for you." He handed Billie a crystal from his side table.

"A copy of what?"

"Vishnu! An electronic genebank of four million species. It's got everything you need to make a cell! The genomes with multiple alleles, the mitochondrial DNA, golgi complexes. Everything! It's all there!" He removed a crystal from the data port and inserted another.

Billie sat down slowly, in shock. Four million species. The animals! She stared at Arnim busily working his console four arms at a time.

He turned to Billie. "There. We have core storage, two alternate files, and three crystals. Now tell me about the computer room."

Billie quickly described the dark room, the power panels; her investigation of the rooms, the consoles — the movement they had felt. "Artemis. Bubble mode," said Billie. She pointed to the tower and antenna, which rose above the genebank. "Did you notice this?"

Arnim shook his head. "They must have left the system set up so all you had to do was turn the power on, and it would transmit."

Billie thought of the paper on the console. "Just a sec," she said as she bounced back into the cargo hold. The fragments were sitting on the cabinet where she had left them. She brought the handful back to the bridge.

"Make that little side table you had before," she instructed Arnim. He touched a panel and the table sprouted from the bottom side of his chair. Billie went over and started arranging the paper on the table. She was a little surprised at how fragile it was. The word had fractured in the middle. She found the first syllable and set it aside. She turned more pieces and there it was:

"Iap" rip "tus".

"It was sitting beside one of the consoles," Billie said.

Arnim leaned over to examine the paper, then looked nervously back at her. "Iapetus," he said. "One of Saturn's moons. Maybe they moved the genebank there. It doesn't matter with the data we have now. Maybe there is more data there. It doesn't matter. I have so much to do as it is. We can't use a piecemeal system anymore. We need automated systems, and centres, for each ecology. Four million species! Oh Billie, do you realize what this means?"

Billie couldn't help but laugh. His joy and enthusiasm were contagious. Arnim was running in half a dozen directions at once. She leaned back smiling, thinking about the beaten child-creature she had tucked into bed yesterday. All at once she felt very slow and prosaic, stalwart even. There was no way she could follow or match the wild mood swings Arnim went through. No way she would want to.

"Are you hungry?" Billie asked during a momentary lull.

"Food?! How can you think of food at a time like this? Four million species!"

"I'm hungry," Billie shrugged.

Arnim slowed down for a second. "Sure let's eat!" he enthused, unexpectedly changing directions. "We'll have a feast!" He jumped up and caught himself just before he hit the ceiling.

Billie laughed. "Artemis. Window mode," she said and followed Arnim back to the food dispensers. This should be interesting, she thought, a feast of nutritional supplements.

As it turned out, Arnim hardly ate at all. He was too busy talking. He made plans in the air for a trip to Iapetus. He discussed no less than three different types of automated systems he and the Repops could deploy. He considered how Vishnu would change the politics of homo superior. He discussed meanwhile, the nutritional contents of each of the bars and bubbles Billie tasted, and he went on about the completion virus and the unique delivery system the unknown faction had used on the Machines. That gave him a new focus for a minute, and he started devising different methods to clean up the nanoslag.

Billie meanwhile sat and ate in silence, from time to time offering Arnim another taste to try. Of all the things that might have happened, she mused almost fondly.

Suddenly she thought of the radio source. "Do you think there might be anyone still alive out here?" she interrupted.

Arnim stopped cold and considered the question. "The probability is vanishingly thin," he answered. "Why?"

"Well, I was just thinking about that radio source."

"Oh yeah. I'd forgotten all about that. Artemis are you still receiving a signal from that radio source?"

"Negative," stated the ship. "The source is now over the horizon."

"Artemis. Play back log recording of the signal," said Arnim.

A hiss of radio noise filled the hold — a series of beeps, whoops and burbles, then a soft female voice speaking in a language Billie did not know. She looked at Arnim and raised her eyebrows. Arnim shook his head. After more radio noise, the voice switched to another language. Billie and Arnim stared at each other frowning.

"Artemis analyze for newlang, English or translatable voice segments."

There was a pause, a little bit of radio noise, and then the soft female voice said, "Hello. Can you hear me? Is anyone there?"

Billie jumped up and yelled, "I have heard this before. In the Machine City. The avatar played this message."

Arnim became very still. Billie looked at him quickly. He was afraid, she saw with some surprise. Another aspect of the Ultra became clear to her. He lived in fear. She sat slowly in front of Arnim. "We've got to go and see who it is."

"It's a machine, a recording. Nobody has spoken those languages since before the war," hissed Arnim.

"Well then, we'd better go and see if we can tell who sent it," replied Billie doing her best to be cheerful and upbeat. "Do you think it is from the asteroid belt, or maybe Iapetus?"

Arnim just looked at Billie. "What if it is dangerous?"

"Fine. I'll go and look at it. You stay inside and monitor."

Arnim considered the proposition. "Okay, but before we do anything, I want to radio a copy of the genebank data back to earth. Just in case anything happens to us. That data is paramount."

"Deal," said Billie and reached over to shake hands. She suddenly could not decide which hand to take and started laughing. "Let's go," she managed to squeeze out.

It was an enthusiastic Billie and a nervous Arnim that bounced and dragged, respectively, back to the bridge.

"Artemis. Lunar holo. Show us the radio source position." Arnim walked through the holo and sat in his throne.

Billie stayed back at the hatch. "Artemis. Did you record any visual images of the radio source?"

A display opened on the side wall opposite from her seat. Arnim swung around to look at it. The view was from the side and at some height. Nothing was visible.

"Artemis. Magnify and enhance," said Arnim. Still there was nothing visible. Whatever the radio source was, it was small.

Arnim snorted and bent back over his console. Billie went and sat down. "Both the Himalayas and . . . " he broke off, seeming to think better of it. "Two sites will soon be visible from near that source." He looked quickly at Billie. "Sit down and hang on."

The Artemis rose slowly and then the main engines fired. "She's not really designed for this kind of hopping around," said Arnim half-apologetically, over the roar of the engines.

Billie looked at the holo. "Artemis. Show our location on the holo." The moon expanded and a small red triangle with a pale green flight path appeared. She watched their progress. It did not take long. The engines stopped and it was suddenly very quiet."Artemis. Zoom in on the radio source," said Arnim as they drifted slowly toward the location. It became clear the reason they could not see anything, was because there was practically nothing to be seen. A thin pole rose at a slight angle from the side of a small hill.

"Artemis. Transparent mode. One to one magnification." said Arnim, as the ship landed about five hundred metres from the pole. He swung his chair around to Billie. "I can send one data stream now, but we need to wait for the world to revolve the other location into view."

Billie nodded.

"Meanwhile, Artemis. Record and archive all signals from the object. Move a copy of all previous signals from the logs to archival storage as well. Constant video monitoring. Alert status three." He stood up as he spoke.

"Acknowledged," replied the ship.

After Arnim had left the bridge, Billie said, "Artemis. Let me listen to it."

"Decrease the volume." Billie sat gazing at the object.

"Genebank data stream transmitted and acknowledged," announced the ship, after a few minutes.

Billie listened to the stream of languages. It was like a recording. The same voice spoke briefly in each of an imponderably long sequence, all the while cut and interspersed with the odd radio hiss, squeals and background noises.

"Hola. Esta cualquier persona alla? Puede usted entedimiento?"

More noise.

"Ciao. A chiunque la? Potete sentirli?

More noise.

"Ola. Esta qualquer um ali? Podc voca entedimiento?"

More noise.

"Artemis. Do you recognize the non-voice parts?" asked Billie.

"Negative. No known modulation or encoding." Billie sat back and listened with her eyes shut. She was intensely curious.

An hour later, Artemis announced, "Radio contact with Khatmandu established."

And a short while after that, Arnim returned to the bridge. Without speaking he bent over his console, then sat back and watched. After a minute, he looked back at Billie with a wry smile. "There are a few petabytes of data, and with the forward error correction . . ."

Billie nodded. She didn't care. In a minute or an hour, she would go and see. There had to be some sign, some indication of the spire's origin. She would find it. She watched and waited with a hunter's patience.

"Okay. You're good to go," said Arnim after a couple of minutes. Billie took a deep breath and headed into the back, Arnim following her. She quickly fitted the flowsuit belt around her waist, moving her belt pouch to the side. She fitted the wrist controls on her forearms and turned the suit on. She spread her arms and lifted her legs to help the suit form as she had done before.

At the airlock, Arnim said. "I'll be monitoring you, but be careful." He emphasized the words be and careful.

Billie smiled. "Don't worry. I'll just take a look and then you can plan where you're going besides Iapetus." She gave him a big grin, hit the helmet button and stepped into the airlock. The interior door flowed shut. After a slight delay, the exterior door flowed open. Billie stepped out onto the surface. The sun was right in front of her. For a second she was caught once again by the stark beauty of the lunarscape, but she turned determinedly toward the radio spire. It stood directly in front of the ship and she set a curving path to approach from the side with the sun behind her.

"Hello Arnim."

"Yes."

"Just checking. I still don't see anything." The radio source looked just like a pole stuck at an angle in the side of dusty little hill. There was a shallow base. Billie drew nearer and walked all the way around the object. The pole extended about five metres, at a slight angle because of the hill. The base was circular, about three metres in diameter. She could not see how far down the base might have extended, but there was no dirt pushed up beside it.

"There's not a mark on it that I can see."

Her second time around, on the side away from the Artemis, something tiny glinted on the pole like a facet on a grain of sand catching the sun. Billie froze.

"Wait a minute. There's something reflecting on the pole. I'm going to take a closer look."

Billie stepped on the base. Nothing happened. She looked around quickly and then focused on the section of the pole which had glinted. She started searching through her suit menu, looking for a way to magnify the display. She took another step.

◆

From where Arnim sat in the pilot's chair, it looked like Billie was instantaneously enveloped in a large silver egg. He lost radio contact and the biostatus display from Billie's suit went flatline.

"Artemis. Play that back in slow motion. Full monitor of suit status in a separate screen." He sat and watched Billie move ever so slowly onto the pad. He saw where she was looking through her suit control screens, then a flash of rainbow colours caught his eye. And there was a silver egg.

He looked back at the outside display. Nothing had changed. "Artemis. Slow that down some more. Played back at the slower rate, he saw a spectrum of colours radiate across the floor and as the colours spread, the walls of the egg rose. "Artemis.

Thumbnail in sequence and identify by time stamps." He looked at the display in shock. The entire envelopment had taken only microseconds.

✦

Billie felt a slight vibration underfoot. There was a flash of colour, and then she was inside an egg shape. For a second she was stunned to immobility. The walls were shifting through a spectrum of colours, at first very quickly, then more slowly red blue yellow mauve bands moved across the floor and up the walls of the egg. Screens began to form all around the interior and the colours faded. Billie began to hear sound filtered through her suit, not via radio. There was air. It was the same cacophony of voices she had heard in the Artemis, except these were simultaneous. She was the focus of a multimedia show. She slowly walked around looking at the screens. Each was in a different language — scripts she did not recognize, languages she could not read.

Hello was displayed on one screen and Billie reached out and touched it. Abruptly the cacophony stopped.

Through her suit, the same soft female voice said, "You may remove your suit and helmet."

"Like bloody hell," muttered Billie and was surprised to see her words appear on a screen in front of her. The walls rolled through bands of colour again briefly, and all the other screens disappeared.

"Who are you? What are you doing?" demanded Billie.

"Our name is a song, but we do not expect you to sing. You may call us Xyala's child."

"Yeah, yeah," Billie was getting angry. If you can't get a straight answer, maybe you're not asking the right question, she heard Finian say in her mind's ear. "What do you want? What are you doing here?" She cast about for a direction, a way to approach this entity.

"The Communion does not want for anything. We have come to offer you citizenship," replied the voice.

Billie was puzzled. "Citizenship? Citizenship in what?" Billie asked.

"Perhaps citizenship is inaccurate. Integration might be better."

Billie felt blank. She was not getting useful information. "Where are you from?" she asked.

"We do not know," replied the voice. "We were not given that information."

The entity, the probe, the creature? Billie was not at all sure what she was dealing with. "You are here to offer us integration." She followed the trail of breadcrumb clues. "What does that mean?"

"Perhaps integration is not a sufficiently accurate word either. Absorption might be better."

Billie had the sudden impression she was talking to a machine designed to draw her out. "Who made you?" she inquired.

"As I told you, we are Xyala's child."

They had gone full circle! What was the right question? What did she really want to know? "Were you made by a human?"

"Many species are joined in whole."

"Many? How many? How many of you are there?"

"There is only one."

A dread fear raised the hair on the back of Billie's neck. "How can that be? You said there were many species."

"They are one now, as you will be."

Once again colours radiated from the pole outwards around the shell. This time the floor moved. It wavered and rose to envelop her legs. She couldn't move. She was trapped like a fly in amber.

"Hey! What are you doing?" yelled Billie.

"Xyala welcomes your separateness."

"Not if I have anything to do with it!" snarled Billie. She reached for her pouch and realized it was inside her suit. Again she was looking through the damned control screens in a panic. <Pouch>, <pocket>, <emergency procedures>, <male>, <urination> There it was! The floor material had risen to mid-thigh. Warning messages flashed across the bottom of her field of vision, giving readouts of rising external pressure.

Billie didn't want to open her suit, but she had to get the Reclaim. She locked her eyes on <Execute> and a seam opened in the front of her suit. She bent over to reach inside. The shimmering alien material was right in front of her eyes. She felt the pouch, then the crystals. She grabbed a handful and pulled her arm out. The shimmering silver metal approached her waist. She felt a sharp pain in her groin.

A red light flashed in the corner of her eye. "Suit integrity breached," a flat voice stated in her ear. She had three crystals. She squeezed and scratched the Reclaim with time zero. The crystal fell achingly slow in the lunar gravity.

A flash of light put her in the middle of a tornado. A rising squeal of radio interference assaulted her ears. Nothing was solid. She started to fall. Caught herself. The Reclaim did not recognize her suit. More red lights began to flash. For a second the helmet's exterior view shut off. An intense pain shot through Billie's foot. It was incredibly cold, then she couldn't feel it any more. She could not breath. The egg was gone. A mass of vibrating spheres enveloped her to the knees. She could not breath. Her suit was being stripped away, turned into motes which could not fly because there was no atmosphere. The vibrating horde began to stream downhill in slow motion. She could not breath. The display stopped. Her arm was free. She was naked on the moon. She saw the Artemis briefly, then collapsed sideways. Her lungs spasmed. She could not breath.

✦

Arnim sat gazing at the silver egg from the pilot's chair. For five minutes nothing changed, then he saw a shimmer of movement and as he watched in amazement, the egg dissolved. In the middle of a vibrating mass of nano iridescent material, Billie stood waving her arms, struggling to stay upright. For a few seconds he regained radio contact with the suit. It was breached. The biosigns were fragmentary, erratic.

As he watched, he saw Billie stripped naked from head to foot. Exposed to the lunar environment, she stood for a second then collapsed. Around her body, tiny shapes warred and streamed, flowing away downhill until finally, only the body was left lying on the side of the hill.

Arnim was stunned. What had happened? He sat panting on his big chair, trying to get a hold of his emotions. To his amazement, Billie sat up. He saw her shoulders convulse and she threw up. Then she turned and collapsed once again.

Arnim's immediate reaction was to want to run away, but there was nowhere to go. The body did not move again for a minute, then once more it convulsed and Billie tried to sit up. Something very strange was going on. Arnim sat and watched the body revive itself, struggle momentarily and cease moving two more times.

He was in a bind. He was terrified. He did not want to be exposed to wild nano, and yet he felt he owed the girl. Above and beyond it all, he was curious. What had happened in the egg? Nobody knew that humans were using nano. Maybe it was from the probe. He had to find out.

He got up and went into the back. From one of the cabinets on the wall, he picked up a pair of wrist control panels. He slipped on the panels and leaned back against a large block on the wall. He pressed on. Around him formed a large waldo. Made of the same flowmetal as the suits, but proportionally larger and heavier, the waldo was an industrial strength version designed for hazardous environments; its failsafe systems could handle any known wild nano. Of the six arms, only two ended in hands. The others had been left as tools and Arnim did not bother to change them.

He moved to the cargo portal and using eye commands from the suit instructed Artemis to open the airlock. In the lunar gravity and with its power amplification effect, the suit was comfortable and moved easily, even though he could feel his increased mass. As he approached the human's body, it moved once more.

He stood over the thin girl, looking down. Her eyes opened and an expression Arnim could not decode filled her face. She died almost immediately. He quickly eyed his tools menu and using his two middle arms, generated a cupped tray which he used to scoop the body from the surface.

In the corner of his eye, a message flashed. "Wild nano detected. Neutralized." He started back towards the Artemis. While he was carrying it, the lively corpse spasmed yet again.

He quickly opened the exterior cargo portal using the suit menus, and stepped inside. "Artemis. Decontamination procedure. Nano and non-terrestrial agents possible. Execute," Arnim commanded by voice. The exterior airlock closed.

"Acknowledged," replied the ship. Thirty seconds later replying, "No foreign elements detected. The human is dead."

"Artemis. Verify decontamination protocol complete," instructed Arnim.

"Complete," replied Artemis.

He looked through his screens and selected a suit command to enclose the cupped tray on which the human lay.

"Artemis. Decontamination procedure. Nano and non-terrestrial agents possible. Execute," Arnim repeated.

"Acknowledged," replied the ship, and shortly after, "Still no foreign elements detected."

"Artemis. Lift off to lunar orbit, low acceleration."

"Acknowledged."

Arnim felt the ship move, a slight force he could ignore pulled him back. "Artemis. Initialize the medunit. Prepare for full isolation mode." Inside the ship, one of the several cabinets along the cargo hold flowed into a diagnostic bed; another transformed itself into an attached medical console.

"System ready."

Arnim eyed the command to open the interior airlock. He stepped inside and walked slowly to the medical unit. He laid the covered tray on the diagnostic bed and stopped. He eyed the suit command to create an emergency exit in the back of the waldo. He stepped back and down from the immobile device, then moved well away from the medunit.

"Artemis. Full isolation mode for waldo and medunit. Execute."

A flowmetal wall rose around the medunit and the waldo still holding the tray with the body inside. It reached from ceiling to floor, completely enclosing the space.

"Artemis. Give me a window to the medunit, and prepare to shut down the waldo. Continue monitoring for nano and non-terrestrial agents."

"Acknowledged." The wall between Arnim and the body appeared to become transparent.

"Artemis. Waldo off," said Arnim and the large device flowed down into a cube on the floor with the control pads on top. The body of the human lay on the diagnostic bed with a sheath wrapped about her torso. The medical readout showed she was dead. He turned away wondering just what had happened.

Arnim jumped when he heard Billie gasp. She moaned. "Artemis. Medical readout and duplicate console on the isolation wall." In disbelief he saw the diagnostic display of an erratic heart-beat, hyperventilation, an abnormally low body temperature.

Billie was holding her head. She opened her eyes and saw him. "Water," she said. The heart went flatline on the display above. While Arnim watched in stunned silence, she died again. He was startled into action. He went to the duplicate medconsole, and instructed oxygen and intravenous fluids. From the base of the medical unit two extrusions reached up and wrapped around Billie's forearms.

She seemed to swell. In a few minutes, she again gasped a deep breath and tried to sit up. She shook her arms and the medunit released her. She projectile vomited an amazingly long stream of black purulent material along the isolation room. It bounced and sprayed into the air, slowly falling to the rear wall.

Billie was shivering. Arnim instructed the medunit to raise its temperature. She held her head and moaned. Billie looked up at Arnim and said. "Thank you." She settled back into a sudden deep sleep. The medunit again wrapped extrusions around her arms and began feeding her fluids and nutrients.

"Artemis. Continue monitoring for wild nano and unknown organisms. Start a complete medical scan of the subject."

"Acknowledged."

Arnim watched Billie for a minute, troubled and confused, then he went to the bridge. He looked down at the moon. The ship had lifted up and away from the radio site and without direction was headed into a polar orbit. Briefly he calculated a correction to bring their orbit back over the radio source. Working remotely, Arnim prepared the medunit for acceleration, and boosted into higher orbit. He gathered high resolution multispectral scans of the region by the radio source. The Artemis orbited once around the moon and as the ship came around the far side, a short burn brought them into an earth trajectory.

"Artemis. Contamination scan report."

"No dangerous organisms detected. No wild nano detected," replied the ship.

"Continue monitoring."

"Acknowledged."

The isolation block around the medunit extended two thirds of the way across the hold, and as Arnim passed back and forth between the bridge and the back of the ship, he watched Billie as she slept. The Artemis still detected nothing untoward and slowly he relaxed.

✦

Billie did not so much awake as drift on the waters of forgetfulness and gently nudge a sandy shore. She opened her eyes and did not recognize the place. It was dark; the only light coming from the diagnostic display. She was starving and she couldn't move her arms. In a sudden inchoate panic, Billie struggled to sit up, pulling and yanking on the medunit arms. The medunit released her, receding smoothly into the base below and for her exertions, Billie drifted up from the bed.

Freefall. We're in space, she thought. As she drifted toward the wall above bits and pieces came teasingly back — the radio source, the language screens, the alien device, absorption, the suit alarms, Artemis from outside, forever falling night. She bumped into the ceiling.

"Artemis. Lights." The illumination bothered her eyes. "Not so bright."

Billie started the ritual. "I recognize these hands." She reached out to push away from the wall and looked at her hands in dismay. They were a child's hands. They were tiny. She didn't recognize her hands!

Suddenly she remembered Finian talking about the alternate senses of the ritual. Even if your new body seems unfamiliar to you, it is vital to accept your strange new flesh, he had said. The word recognize can also mean acknowledge and accept. This intention is buried in the ritual for those who might need it. Billie examined herself. She looked at her hands, her feet, her breasts. This is my body now, she thought, and started the Ritual When Alone once more.

"I recognize these hands.

I recognize these feet.

I know this heart, and it is good.

I know this body head to toe.

I am this flesh.

I am whole.

I am this flesh.

I know this body head to toe.

I know this heart, and it is good.

I recognize these feet.

I recognize these hands."

At first she had to think about it, but somewhere in the middle the words started coming automatically. The ritual had done what it was supposed to do. Billie's hunger demanded attention. She had no food, no water. She broke off.

"Artemis. I need food and water."

"Isolation protocol in effect," replied the ship.

Isolation? Billie pondered that. "Artemis. Is Arnim on board?"

"Yes."

"Can I talk to him? No wait. Can I see and talk to him at the same time?"

"Yes."

Billie waited. Nothing happened. Then she realized she had only asked a question as far as the machine was concerned.

"Artemis. Where is Arnim?"

"Arnimalayandagoton is presently on the bridge."

"Artemis, make an audio and video connection to the bridge console."

Arnim was in the cockpit wondering about his cargo when Billie spoke. "Hey let me out of here!" Her face filled a screen on his console. The clever girl had got Artemis to start conference mode.

"Oh. Hello, Billie. How are you?"

"I'm starving and I need to pee. Let me out."

"I can't do that."

"Why not?"

"I've put you in isolation. You are now hazardous cargo."

"What do you mean?" Her brow puckered.

"Artemis detects wild nano infiltrating your skeletal structure."

"Oh that's just Restart," said Billie smiling disingenuously. "I'm not any more dangerous than I was before."

"Restart? Is that what you call it?"

"So you can let me out now. Right?" offered Billie hopefully. To her dismay, a toilet unit unfolded itself from the rear corner of the room.

"No. I will not expose myself. I will take you back to your people and let you go. Be glad of that."

The screen shut off abruptly and Billie pulled back, startled and vexed. She was hungry. It was almost like being back in the cell. When Billie finished using the toilet, a compartment opened in the side wall with an array of food supplements inside. She picked them all up and put them on the bed. They jostled, bounced and floated slowly up toward the back wall. Billie shrugged and started to eat.

A screen appeared on the far wall at the foot of the medunit. Arnim appeared. "Ah Billie, look." He was apologetic. "I want you to understand."

Billie looked at him trying to gauge her options. "Thanks for the food," she said, setting a water bulb aside, and breaking into a wide grin. "Is there any chance of getting some clothes, and maybe my stuff?"

Arnim nodded. "Of course," he said and the screen winked off. A couple of minutes later, Billie's poncho and shoulder bag irissed through the wall. A couple of minutes after that, an outfit of silvery Ultra material appeared as well. She was trying to make head and tail of the Ultra garment when Arnim popped up on the wall screen again.

"I thought you might have trouble with that. Look. Do this." He ran his thumbnail down his chest, pressing moderately hard. The material of his shirt split open where he had pressed. "And you put it together like this." He overlapped the divided halves and ran his palm along the seam. The silvery material annealed and joined leaving no visible juncture. "There are control pads as well, but the default behaviour is usually sufficient."

Billie took off her poncho and fitted the Ultra suit as best she could. She had to seal the sides where a couple of extra arms would have gone, but the material turned out to be quite malleable and comfortable. Once she had it on, the silver suit pulled and adjusted itself to her form.

"Thanks," she said.

Arnim nodded.

"Where are we?"

Arnim looked away momentarily. The front and rear walls of the isolation unit became screens. They were falling back toward the earth.

"How long until we arrive?" she asked.

"Five hours plus."

"Oh, I didn't realize I'd slept that long." Billie nabbed another food bar. She was ravenous. "So what did you want me to understand?" she asked feeling a little self-satisfied at the ease with which she was able to direct the Ultra.

"Look at this," said Arnim. A large screen opened on the side wall and his screen closed. It was a view of the moon seen from lunar orbit. Billie recognized the pattern of craters around the radio spire. Another overlapping view with a blowup of the site appeared. Around the bottom of the hill where she had died, were hundreds of small silver eggs — all different sizes. Billie gaped.

"Any idea what that is?" asked Arnim as his screen reappeared. Evidently he had been watching her, just not showing himself, Billie realized.

"No," she replied shaking her head in a daze.

He looked at her intently. "You'd better tell me what happened inside that thing."

"Couldn't you see?" asked Billie.

"No. I lost contact when the entity enveloped you."

"My memory is fuzzy." She quickly described the colours, the language screens, the alien conversation, the suit alarms and incorporation. "When it started to envelop my legs, I decided I had to use Reclaim, but . . . "

"Wait a minute," interrupted Arnim. "What exactly is Reclaim?"

Billie described the crystals Finian had programmed to fill the warehouse of materials and elements.

"That must leave a lot of carbon fibre laying around," observed Arnim.

"No, the nanobots deposit their load and fly on to the Arctic, as part of a carbon sequestering process."

"An active containment system," Arnim mused aloud, "but surely there are accidents."

Billie laughed. "I remember once seeing a very scared naked four-year-old standing and crying where his parents' kitchen had been, but Reclaim will not touch a living cell."

Arnim gazed at her thoughtfully. "Our first contact with an alien lifeform, ever, and you destroy their probe with wild nano."

Billie stared right back at him. "Well, yup. That's about the size of it. And if it tried to incorporate me again, I'd do the same thing again."

Arnim couldn't help but smile, for her forthrightness if not for the irony of the situation. He killed the videoconference to think. For thousands of years, humans had dreamed of and yearned for life among the stars, and the first contact yields a field of silver eggs on the moon. It was ironic, almost perverse. He shook his head. They would have to be investigated. Safely. Robotically. A jury would be struck. He thought of the genebank. Oh there was so much work to do.

A screen popped open on his console. "Hey! You said you wanted me to understand something, but you didn't say what."

Arnim glanced at Billie in some exasperation. "Yes. But not now, I need to think. Artemis. Privacy mode."

Billie's screen disappeared. Arnim considered Iapetus, a search of the solar system, the committees to be struck, who was available, how few were willing and able to do the work, all the while avoiding the context — what he had to tell this human and could barely acknowledge as true himself. His mind recoiled and he busied himself with orbital mechanics, the removal of nanoslag — the solvable problems.

✦

Billie put the isolation unit in bubble mode. She floated between the images of the earth and moon, eating a nutritional supplement bar. She couldn't get the image of the silver eggs out of her mind. They reminded her of something she couldn't quite remember. Silently she drifted and ate. She didn't know how many times she had died on the moon — she didn't want to know. All she knew was she was incredibly weak and tired and hungry. The rich food made her drowsy and she drifted lazily in and out of sleep.

In a funny-odd way the isolation unit made leaving easier. She was already separate; now it was just a matter of distance. Billie thought of all the ways she had seen Arnim — the overbearing superior Ultra, the co-conspirator, the hyperactive child, the fearful stranger, the distraught creature she had tucked into bed, the planner with a head full of ideas. She would never have guessed Ultras were like that.

An inventory of all the things she would like to take home began to form in her mind — the silver Ultra clothes, a smart suit, some flowmetal. In sudden alarm she thought, I lost the genebank holo data crystal with my pouch belt back on the moon. I'll have to get another. She turned and looked at the Earth drawing ever closer. Four million species! Perhaps someone in the Water Clan knew something about molecular biology. She closed her eyes and drifted.

Sometime later, Arnim's screen opened on the ceiling overhead. "Billie. Excuse me."

Billie opened her eyes and looked at Arnim. He was upside down. She was upside down. She pushed off the back wall toward the medunit. Effectively that orientation defined down for her, even if things did fall another direction.

"We don't have a lot of time," he began. "And this is difficult, so let me get it out." He paused, and changed direction. "Have you ever wondered why you never see Ultras where you live?"

"Oh yes. We sit around talking about nothing else." Billie stated.

Arnim didn't rise to the bait. He was intent on what he was saying. "I tell you this because I think you humans need to know. We leave you alone because you are the only ones."

"The only what?"

"The only humans alive. We know. We have looked. If there are any other humans in the solar system, they are hiding very well." Arnim stopped. "There is that, and then there is the fear."

"Fear?"

"You have to understand. We were created by humans for human purposes. Each type of superior you see was designed for a specific job. We are like idiot savants, autistics really good at certain things, terrible at others." He raised his six arms as if in demonstration. "Do you understand what I am saying?" Arnim looked at Billie with a painful pleading expression.

"As far as it goes," said Billie hesitantly. "Ummmm no," she concluded.

"We were made with built-in control mechanisms. If you knew the right command phrases, you could make me do anything you wanted. We are vulnerable to you and the easiest way to ensure you never learn to use those commands is to avoid you altogether. Those marker poles in the desert are there to protect us, not you."

Billie sat back startled and Arnim continued. "There is more." For a long minute there was only silence. Billie waited for it.

"We are not viable," said Arnim simply. The statement hung in the air like an emotional black hole. He seemed to catch himself, and continued in his professorial mode, "Of course, we have the vats. We know how to make and use the hardware. We keep trying to find a way out of the trap your ancestors laid and made of us. We keep trying to create new variants." Arnim fixed Billie with a penetrating glare. "What 'you' would call new Ultras." He put an emphasis on the word 'you' that made Billie squirm with the bitterness. "Perhaps we will succeed. Some are still trying; others have given up. The design of new lifeforms is more of an art than a science. The results have not always been good or useful. Unfortunately there does not seem to be a gene for wisdom."

He stopped and regarded Billie, but she was not about to distract him in any way. She had slipped into the quiet mode she usually assumed when others acted strangely. An indecipherable look flitted across Arnim's face.

"You cannot build a society of brilliant and eccentric misfits alone. The Old Ones wanted to increase our intelligence. And they did. They also wanted to keep us under control. And they did that too. Look at it this way. If you could design any life form you want, what characteristics would you give your own children? And what characteristics would you give a worker in your factory? We are the factory androids that happened not to be targeted in the biowar. Oh, we have the boosted immune systems. We are not susceptible to many of the classical diseases, but we are flawed by design. We live in fear. And your ancestors made us this way!"

Arnim gazed at her accusingly for a moment. Then he took another right angle turn and asked, "Do you know what we call ourselves?"

Billie shook her head.

Arnim laughed. "We don't. There is no us. No group awareness. The Old Ones wanted us smart, not cohesive, and we have never found a way to undo that predisposition. Geneteching social skills is not nearly as straightforward as changing an organ or increasing symbolic intelligence."

Billie waited him out. She had heard this story before with a slightly different twist.

A look of deep despair returned to Arnim's face. "You have to understand how it is for us. We who were tools — not even slaves — are now masters of a brave new dead world. Imagine you are completely free with nothing and no one to look over your shoulder. No parents, no law, no god, no community, nothing. You are completely free to do or be whatever you want. That is where we find ourselves. We are condemned to a freedom few can comprehend and it has had terrible consequences. A kind of madness has come over us."

Arnim seemed to lose himself in a private horror, and then extract himself slowly and delicately. "That is what I mean when I say we Ultra are not viable — not viable biologically or socially. I do not think we will last for long." He looked away, but did not break the connection. After a few seconds he added, "And that is also why you need to know about the genebank."

Billie floated between the earth and the moon watching the Ultra's mood — grief, bitter anger, fear, horror and despair, all tied up with other feelings she could not understand. As soon as he looked back at her, she said, "I lost my copy of the genebank."

Arnim smiled. "Yes. I realize. I made another one for you." He picked up a holo crystal to show her. Over the videoscreen audio Billie heard Artemis announce, "Five minutes until orbital insertion burn."

Arnim looked at her. "I'll adapt the medunit to an acceleration couch. Get ready." He turned back to his console and calculations.

Billie didn't know how to ask and decided she might just as well be direct. "Arnim. Can I have a flowsuit? It would be really useful."

Arnim glanced back at her briefly. "You may as well have the waldo."

Billie looked puzzled and Arnim explained, "That's the big block beside the medunit. It's a flowsuit and more. As a matter of fact you can have the whole isolation unit and everything it contains. I would just have to destroy it all anyway."

The Return

Nitrosomonas europaea

"Nitrosomonas europaea, *an obligate chemolithoautotroph, was among the first prokaryotes sequenced because its key position in the nitrogen cycle was realized even before genetic sequencing became ordinary. In concert with several other 'nitroso' aerobic bacteria, such as* Nitrosovibrio, Nitrosolobus, Nitrosospira, Nitrosococcus *and* Nitrosococcus, *the* Nitrosomonas *use ammonium as an energy source by first oxidizing it to nitrite. Targeting this prokaryote is widely considered the single most egregiously destructive act of the biowar."*

— Wilhemina Featherstone III

◆

IT ALL SEEMED TO HAPPEN SURPRISINGLY FAST. Artemis braked into earth orbit. After a bumpy re-entry, they landed. For a while nothing happened. Billie tried to contact Arnim, but he had engaged privacy mode and Artemis wouldn't interrupt him. The medunit and medconsole reverted suddenly to standby flowmetal cubes. Then the isolation unit started to flow down and Billie found herself standing outside the ship. The isolation unit, and all its contents including her, had been extruded whole through the side of ship.

They never said goodbye. Billie felt that Arnim was watching, but she did not see him again. *Perhaps I am too dangerous now that I know about human control*, she thought. The Artemis rose and flew away to the south. Billie waved once and briefly felt funny-sad. She stood watching it disappear with growing detachment.

It was baking hot. The sun was burning down from a mid-afternoon sky and she had no hat. The Ultra cloth, while comfortable held the heat. Billie looked around quickly. She was beside an Ultra pole, about fifty kilometres south of the Mission. She was in the oven of summer.

I guess the only way I'll get this stuff back to the Mission, is to use the Waldo, Billie decided. She was weak and tired, but had no other choice. She fitted the wrist controls on her arms and turned it on. The size and power of the device was a surprise, but inside it was just like a flowsuit. She was cool and calm and she only had the three flowmetal cubes to carry to the Mission.

She had no food, but she had water. She turned the waldo helmet and hands off and pulled her old water bottle out of her shoulder bag. *Now this is educated water*, she thought with a laugh, thinking how far it had travelled and remembering the old man back at the Village who always asked her after a season's run "did you get an education?" The mass of the waldo arm threw her motion off a little and she spilled some water on the dusty sand. She looked down and the splat where the water had landed was already drying.

Somehow that sight galvanized her into action. She quickly put the water bottle away, restored the waldo helmet and hands and started searching the control menus for a way to carry the three flowmetal cubes. In the end she formed a platform above her shoulders, shortened two arms and turned the other pair into cargo straps. She was heavy, seven hundred and eight-eight kilograms according to the suit, and had to step carefully — with elephant feet — but she was in balance and ready to go.

Billie started toward the Mission. She quickly discovered she had to generate a heat removal subsystem when an alarm popped up on her display. Fortunately it was preconfigured and happened almost automatically. She also discovered that she could scan three hundred sixty degrees in multiple wavelengths, which she set the suit to do in a small screen off to the side of her field of vision. The footsteps she left were monstrous — large and deep. She barely noticed.

The sun moved into the west. Billie soldiered on. Stopping was not an option. When the sun set, she generated lights on the sides of her helmet and kept going. Using an infrared view and knowing her route well, she was able to make good progress even in the dark.

In the middle of the night, Billie put down her load. She saved the waldo configuration and turned it off. The night air was still quite warm as she lay down on her back. Billie put her arms out on either side and tried to relax. She was all keyed up; she had been pushing herself so hard. She was bone tired, but her nerves were on edge and sleep was far away. Images of the last few days passed through her mind unbidden — the genebank, the silver eggs, the magic moment when Arnim had put the bridge in bubble mode. Suddenly she was not lying on the ground; she was spread eagled on the edge of a huge ball spinning through space. Billie felt dizzy. She was falling up! She opened her eyes, and the stars — a blazing path of diamonds across the sky — the stars were not moving. She sighed and let it go. It took a while, but eventually, the gentle waters of Lethe lapped against her feet.

At any rate, my body rested she thought, as she arose in the morning, feeling stiff and cramped. There must be some feedback effect after prolonged use of the suit, she deduced. A sip of water, a rub of her eyes and she was ready. Well, at least as ready as I am ever going to be, she told herself. Billie remembered her mentor Jack saying, 'when starting a difficult task, the first thing you gotta do is build up your enthusiasm.' She chuckled, restored the waldo's travel configuration, picked up the flowmetal cubes and set off toward the Mission.

The waldo's optical system could do magnifications, she discovered, and she watched the blow-up screen for the first sign of the valley ahead. When she did arrive at the southern end, there seemed to be an odd lack of activity. There were no vehicles, no movement, no one in the valley. As she rounded the bend, a couple of kilometres from the Mission, she couldn't see anyone. The valley looked singed, as usually happened this time of year, but there was green, so the pumps were still working. Billie moved slowly utilizing the suit's three–hundred-sixty degree scan mode. It was strange. Usually people swarmed all over the place this time of day. Far down the valley, past the Mission, a raven cawed and spread its wings. Billie zoomed in on the bird sitting at the top of the tallest poplar. It preened with avian aplomb.

Slowly and with mounting dread, Billie approached the Mission. When she got to within twenty metres, the front doors opened and Hannah stepped out holding a rifle. She wasn't about to let anyone, or anything, hurt her children. At the same time Billie heard a voice behind her whisper, "Quiet!" but there was nobody in sight. The ground right in front of the Mission steps was wrong. It looked normal to her eyes, but the infrared showed a rectangle on the ground. A warning "Explosive Detected" flashed across the bottom of her field of vision.

"Who are you? What do you want?" demanded Hannah raising the rifle barrel. Suddenly Billie realized they couldn't see her, just the waldo.

"Hannah. It's me," said Billie, turning off her hands and helmet.

"Billie?" said Hannah in disbelief. Billie put the flowmetal cubes down on the ground and turned the waldo off. The flowmetal transformed itself running down her back and forming a cube beside the others.

"Yup. It's just me."

"Glory sakes, you gave us a scare!"

Billie stood rooted, smiling somewhat hesitantly.

Hannah set the rifle down and walked carefully around the buried explosives. "Heavens. What has happened to you?" asked Hannah as she drew near. She took Billie's hand and searched her face.

"That is a long story," said Billie, "Can I get something to eat?"

Hannah seemed to decide that things were okay then all at once, because she turned and called across the valley. "It's alright. You can come out."

Jorge, the cook and several others Billie did not know by name trickled out of the sheds and the storm shelter. Other rose from the nearby fields. Hannah wrapped her arm around Billie's shoulder and guided her carefully around the rectangle of explosives.

"Don't walk there," she said lightly. "Now come and tell me what has happened to you," She held Billie's hand up looking at it, "and why you are so small." They headed for the kitchen. "You know, the last I heard of you, was when Harmer showed up and said the Ultras had taken you."

Billie looked at Hannah in surprise. "Oh, he came back did he?"

"Yes and that is a long story too. Come on let's eat."

After a large meal and much talk, a snack and more talk, Billie slept in the cool and quiet basement. She slept through the rest of the day and most of the night. Dawn found Billie on the roof with a cup of hot tea, watching the sun rise and the beginnings of the day unfold. The explosives had been removed, she could see by the way the ground was turned. The flow cubes corresponding to the waldo, the medunit and console, and the isolation unit still sat where she had left them. I'll have to get some of that off to Finian, she thought.

The door behind her opened and Hannah emerged.

"Morning."

"Good day." It suddenly occurred to Billie how completely the courtesies had been absent among the Ultras. The sun was just peeking over the edge of the valley.

Hannah looked down over the edge of the building at the flow cubes below. "What are you going to do with them?" She nodded downwards.

"They're for Finian ultimately. The waldo could really be useful. The one block is basically just a room. I thought I'd send him a piece of it to see if I could get his interest."

Hannah laughed. "He's already heard about your little entrance here yesterday. The moccasin telegraph never fails to amaze me. I had three messages from him waiting for me when I got up this morning."

Billie smiled. "Two of the blocks are medical. I thought you might be interested in using them, at least until Finian or somebody figures out that flowmetal and how to program it."

Hannah nodded. A silence intervened as they watched the sun clear the edge of the valley. Billie took a long pull of her hot tea, thought of Arnim's syncaf and syringe pot, and chuckled. She turned to Hannah. "You know I've been thinking about what Arnim said. About the Ultras being afraid of our becoming their masters again."

Hannah looked at her wondering where she was going with this.

"You know the command sequences don't you?" said Billie directly.

Hannah sighed and nodded, looking away, down the valley. "Some of them — the medical subset. Other protocols I did not need to know." She fell silent staring into the distance. In a strangely diminutive voice she whispered, "Some of those creatures were treated terribly. They are right to fear us."

"Yes, but doesn't it strike you as funny that we fear them and they fear us and nothing changes."

Hannah frowned. "Humans always generate ingroups and outgroups. That is part of our programming, done not by imprinted command sequences, but by a couple million years of evolution."

"Yeah, but there is so much we could learn from them." Billie stated with vehemence. She turned to Hannah accusingly, "And you knew! You knew all along. Why didn't you say anything?"

Hannah looked down at her hands, then looked Billie straight in the eye. "Because there are some powers one person should not have over another. I will not see the People turn the Ultras into slaves, into things, the way the Old Ones did."

Billie could not deny the logic or the sentiment. She nodded. "It's just too bad," she said wistfully.

Hannah finished her mug of tea with a flourish. "Yes. It is," she said, "but I am damned if I am going to sit around feeling sorry about the way the world is, about doing the right thing. I have work to do." She turned and went back downstairs.

Billie stared down at the flowmetal cubes. And what is my work now, she wondered. Somebody would have to start with the genebank data. It would be so much better if we could work with the Ultras. Maybe there is a way. She drifted in thought.

✦

Billie took to wandering the valley, while she recovered her strength. The isolation unit went back to Finian. She sent it thinking it wouldn't matter much if he did completely ruin it. She set up the medunit and console for Hannah. The waldo she left in a basement storage room. She kept the control pads with her.

A week later, Harmer showed up. Billie happened to be at the south end of the valley and she saw the drone fly overhead. She walked over to the trail and sat down under a clump of poplar to wait. Harmer woke her by tapping her foot. He was coal black from head to foot, and clothed only in a belt and loincloth.

"So you got away," he said. "You look smaller."

Billie smiled nodding. "I hear you have been patrolling for bugs. Don't they just love the heat?"

Harmer crouched down beside her, one knee on the ground. "It seemed a logical thing to do. I was made for the desert" — Billie was surprised to hear this self description — "and I need to do something useful." Billie was more surprised to hear this sentiment. He seemed to have come to the People's values rather quickly.

She got up and they walked slowly toward the Mission. "Do you know what left this track?" asked Harmer pointing to the waldo prints. Billie smiled and told him the story. Then Harmer told her where he had been patrolling, what he had seen. From her knowledge of the countryside, Billie knew exactly where he had been. It occurred to her that she felt strangely comfortable with this soldier, considering he had killed her once.

The sun was setting that day when Billie and Hannah found themselves together again in the rooftop garden. Harmer was in the park at the back of the building, dangling his fingers in the running water. His skin was getting lighter as the valley slowly darkened. Billie watched him almost fondly, "He is fascinated by running water." Then the afterthought struck her. "He is quieter somehow. Not so edgy."

Hannah nodded. "What with all the excitement of your return, we have not had the opportunity to talk about him."

Billie shrugged and looked at Hannah "What's to talk about?"

"I disabled his implants," said Hannah. Billie's eyes grew wide. "That's why he seems calmer to you. He is no longer being constantly stimulated, driven by military imperatives."

Hannah paused for a second. "You need to understand. I can turn off the machine, but I cannot give him what he never had. His memories of life before the army are ersatz."

Billie digested that. "Does he know?"

Hannah nodded.

"And how did he take that?"

Hannah shrugged. "About as well as can be expected. You have to understand. Some emotional reactions may never be there."

Billie looked up. "Yeah, that's too bad, but — Hey! Wait a minute!" Hannah's grin gave her thought away. "No, Hannah. He treats me like just another soldier. I regret what has happened to him, but there is nothing romantic going on between us."

Hannah gazed at her without expression. "Fine. If you say so. Still, he does have an interesting genome."

Billie snorted. "Then hook him up with some woman from the village who can get pregnant, just don't let your imagination run away with you where I am concerned. I am out of that picture. I am nothing."

"Oh Billie, don't be so hard on yourself. There is more to life than babies and husbands."

"Yeah? Like what?!" Billie spat out the words and immediately regretted it. She put her hand out and touched Hannah's arm. "I know. I know. Do you think I don't tell myself that?" Billie sighed.

Hannah regarded Billie with a weary, beaten expression, then continued, "I think you should take him as an apprentice."

"An apprentice? Why? I don't need any help. I don't need an apprentice." Billie scrambled for a reason to reject the idea. "Hannah, he killed me!"

Hannah laughed. "I know. The Old Ones used to have a saying — if you meet Buddha on the road, kill him. Sounds like an ideal apprentice-teacher relationship to me."

Billie spluttered in objection. "No way. I'm a Ranger, not a teacher. I'll just mess things up and make it worse."

Hannah just listened, let her run out of steam, then said, "This is about him, not you. He needs a teacher, a connection to the People. Besides, things always change. It might be good for you both. Mostly we need to give him time."

"Time for what?" asked Billie.

"Time to decide if he wants to become a person." Hannah looked steadily at Billie. "I want you to understand. He is genmod, almost an Ultra, although he never lived in the mountains. He was created to fight in the desert. I have not discussed Restart with him, and I do not think you should either. Frankly, I do not want to have to put up with a freshly decommissioned Harmer every few decades. He's being cooperative now, because he wants to be Restart imprinted, but whether that will last." Hannah shrugged. "We'll see. We'll give him a few years and see how things work out."

Billie and Hannah argued and discussed and considered until late that night and just when they were slowing down, Harmer came up and they started all over again. In the end Hannah won out.

Billie and Harmer started patrolling the southern wastes together. It was late enough in the year that the Last Bush creek was bone dry. The rats avoided the heat during the day, protecting their moisture. Billie and Harmer stayed well north of the creek zigzagging from well to well. For a while it seemed like old times. Billie introduced Harmer to all the ranch folk, people like the Stirlings. They found lots of bugs, and with Harmer's drone, perhaps more than usual.

They worked easily, if distantly, together. She appreciated his abilities, his desert skills. He sometimes seemed surprised that an ordinary human, a woman at that, could keep up with him, frequently be ahead of him. There was no question of sex. Harmer was unmotivated, was perhaps asexual by design. He certainly had the equipment, as Billie often saw. He treated his genitals like just another part of his body, as casually as one treated an arm or a leg. The lack of inhibition, the lack of attention paid to the proprieties was disquieting. It felt more like depersonalization than freedom to her.

One evening, a month and a half after leaving the Mission, as the shadows grew long and the land crackled and sighed releasing its heat back into the sky, Billie sat with her back against a still warm rock, the ruins of an ancient farm scattered beyond their circle of light, and she watched the half-exposed Harmer lying by the dying embers of their fire. There was nothing remotely attractive about him. He was funny looking and that factory skin was unnerving. So Billie was hard pressed to understand what she was feeling. She cast about for reasons — it was that time of the month, it was being alone with a man, it was the moon. A host of rationalizations passed through her mind. The simple heart of it was she wanted to be held. She wanted someone to put his arms around her and love her. And Harmer was the only one there. It was out of the question.

Billie sat quietly and watched the moon rise in the east. Oh, my silver sister, she thought. A single tear ran down her cheek and she did not wipe it away.

She dreamt that night of silver eggs; awoke in the morning feeling particularly grumpy and irritable. Her period had always been irregular, particularly during the hot, hard summer patrols, but by the second month, Billie knew something was up. Her breasts began to hurt. Her nipples were more sensitive than they had ever been. By that time she and Harmer were heading west again, and Billie decided they should stop in at the Mission.

Hannah wanted to talk about Harmer and it took a while before Billie was able to mention her reason for stopping by. When she did, Hannah took her to the diagnostics room and bade her lie on the Ultra medunit.

"I'm glad to see you using this," said Billie, "at least some good came . . . "

"I don't believe it!" interrupted Hannah.

"What?"

"You're pregnant!"

"That cannot be," said Billie flatly, "I have not had a man since I left the village, and besides, it's impossible." She broke off. Hannah knew precisely the knot of growth she had where she ought to have fallopian tubes.

Hannah looked at her archly. "How long ago is that now?"

"February."

"Hmmm. That's five months ago, and you are at most three along." Hannah paused. "I'll run some more tests. We'll see what more we can find out. Just a minute."

Billie didn't know whether to laugh or leave. As she often did in medical surroundings, she began to feel distant, like just another case. Perhaps it was the medical equipment. She thought of TFM lying on the gurney in that same room.

Hannah fiddled with the medical console. "I saw a sequencing capability here the other day," she spoke as much to herself as to Billie, "but do you think I can find it now. You know, there is so much built into this damn thing. Oh there it is." Hannah reached over and grasped Billie by the shoulder, caught her eye and smiled. She turned back to the medconsole. Billie's attention drifted around the room. Pregnant. She still could not believe it. There had to be a mistake.

Hannah stopped all at once and straightened up. "I don't believe it."

"Hannah! I'm getting tired of hearing you say that!" snapped Billie in vexation. Hannah stared at Billie, surprised by her sharp tone. In a more conciliatory voice, Billie asked "What don't you believe?"

"Parthenogenesis."

"Huh? What's that?"

"Your daughter is you." Hannah turned back to the medconsole. "Come here and see for yourself."

Billie got up and moved in a daze to stand beside Hannah. "See. The sequences are identical." Hannah pointed to two base pair sequences displayed beside each other in graphical and numeric formats. "All of this is identical. Maybe I can get this thing to show us the difference." She started paging through control screens and Billie just floated, watching the strands of DNA scroll by. Abruptly the long spiral molecules all turned green, and the view zoomed out. A clump of red clung near one end of the DNA molecules.

"Oh. There is a difference. There," said Hannah. "Let's see what this is." She bent back over the console. "The X chromosome. See," she turned to Billie, "except for this section of X chromosome, her genetic sequence is the same as yours. No. Let me rephrase that. The level of difference detected is less than the error sampling rate of this device." Hannah slapped the side of the medconsole. "For all intents and purposes, she is your clone. Except I wonder . . ." her voice ran off. "Let's see what these new sections do."

Billie felt at once utterly calm, completely shocked and hungry in a strangely languorous way. Hannah by now had collected her wits and was trying to sequence and analyze the extra X chromosome material. Billie had never seen Hannah in this analytic mode and she gazed at her friend curiously.

"These genes produce different proteins. And this structure is almost like a ribosome, but I have no idea what it might do. Some of these are like neurochemicals." Hannah continued with her analysis, talking to herself softly, while Billie watched in amusement. Suddenly Hannah stopped. "They look designed. Is it possible the Ultras did something to you, while they were interrogating you?"

Billie was surprised. That was a possibility she had not considered. "I don't know. I was drugged right out of it, so I guess it's possible, but why?"

"Not that I know what they might have done to trigger parthenogenesis," continued Hannah, "that is a trick I doubt even they could manage."

The room fell silent as the two women watched the sequencer run through the base pairs once again. The same pattern of green with red near the end was displayed.

Hannah took a deep breath. "Okay, you're pregnant. Okay, there are some anomalous sequences, which I don't understand. They look engineered, but . . . " She began speaking as though she were reciting a checklist. "Billie. You have to make some decisions." They locked eyes.

"Do you want to keep the child?"

"Yes," Billie answered at once without thinking.

"Even though there may be problems?"

"Yes." She was definite.

"There may be problems because of that X chromosome."

"I understand."

"You may lose the child anyway."

"I understand."

Hannah stopped. "Then there is just one last thing. It is still early in your term. You have time to travel to the Village. The midwives are there and there will be other birth mothers."

Billie was gratified to see the wave of joy come into Hannah's face when she replied, "I would rather stay here. I trust you."

Hannah took her hand beaming. "Well. I'll have to get you set up in some better quarters — with a nursery." She turned at once for the door, all business and starch.

"Jorge! Jorge!" she called, "Oh where is that man? He's never around when you need him." She bustled out of the room.

Billie lay back on the medunit and stared at the ceiling. It was wonderful. It was incredible. She had to pee.

The months slipped by. Billie wandered near the Mission gradually being drawn in by the growing presence in her body. She was distressed that her body hurt. She felt awkward and ungainly. The novelty was definitely gone. Who could she complain to? It wasn't fair. It was funny. It was not funny. All her life, Billie had just up and left when she didn't like a situation. You get used to living on nothing and you appreciate the freedom it affords. Now she was the situation. She was stuck. And dammit she always had to pee.

Strangely enough, now that she couldn't run away, she found herself thinking about things more deeply. Always before she had distracted herself with movement. Now she could not run. She spent a lot of time on the rooftop, watching the valley folk and thinking. Her conversations with Arnim played like a tape recording in her sleeping mind's ear. She found herself thinking about restoring the species. It was a worthwhile thing to do, and nobody else was coming forward. Billie thought about it and began to study.

It struck her as strange at first, that none other of the People had taken up the task of learning the ins and outs of molecular biology. The plans for synthesis machines, the artificial wombs, were all stored in the library crystals. Billie immersed herself in the intricacies of the cell, the mitochondrial DNA, the organelles — the mind-boggling complexity of the interactions of genes and protein. Maybe the People's attitude wasn't so strange after all.

Billie sat back wondering if this huge task was really something she wanted to assume and as soon as she asked herself the question, she knew. It was the right thing to do. "Oh, I have so much to learn, so much to do," she gasped. An image of the future flashed through her mind — the years a rising spiral. She would begin with plants. That would be easiest and perhaps most useful. No wombs to deal with. She might have to adapt the plants to the bioplagues still active. And the People farming up north could use the plants she re-created. It would help convince them she wasn't wasting her time.

It would also help, if she could tell them quickly and easily before hand, what she was doing and why. I can no longer be a Ranger, she realized with a pang. I will be something completely new — a Seedmother. She straightened her shoulders and said aloud, "I am Wilhemina Featherstone. My tribe is hunter and my work is Seedmothering."

Jorge happened to be nearby tending the rooftop garden, and he overheard Billie's declaration. For the rest of his many years and many lives, he told people, "I was there the day the first Seedmother dedicated herself."

For Billie it was nothing so dramatic. It was a direction and there was far to go. Not only that. The baby kicked and she had to move. Then she had to pee. She went back downstairs to tell Hannah of her new work.

Harmer took up Billie's patrol. From time to time he stopped in at the Mission, but Billie found it hard to pay any attention to him when the full orchestra of her body's unfolding was so overwhelming. Luckily Hannah seemed to have a way with him, and Harmer spent most of his time with her.

Billie began to have a recurrent dream. She was floating in a field of silver eggs. Sometimes she was herself; sometimes she was an egg. When she was herself, she'd touch one of the eggs and it would open to some incident from the past. She lived again the day her parents disappeared. She met Finian for the first time; made her first trip south of the Ultra poles with Jack the Ranger; travelled again through the Dead City. It wasn't every night, but often enough to make her wonder.

Hannah did not seem concerned. "Is the dream distressing?" she asked, and when Billie said, "No," Hannah went on talking about Harmer's genetic structure. She was wondering if his photosynthetic skin was a dominant trait.

When Billie was about eight and a half months into her term, Hannah Restarted. She and Billie were crossing the big hall one evening, when Hannah cried out and collapsed. Jorge who just happened to be in the front lobby heard the noise and came running. Gently he cradled the dying woman. He looked up at Billie. "It's her heart. It's always her heart, you know." He held Hannah's head to his chest as she died. A couple of minutes later she Restarted. Together Billie and Jorge started the Ritual for Another.

"I recognize these hands.

I recognize these feet . . ."

Hannah's eyes opened. She clasped Jorge's hand and together they finished the ritual.

"I know this heart, and it is good.

I know this body, head to toe.

You are this flesh.

You are whole.

We rejoice you are among us."

Five minutes later, Hannah was a sixty-year-old woman again, bustling about giving orders. Billie watched it all spin by like a dream.

The child was late — nine months, nine and half months. Hannah was starting to worry. Then one night Billie was awakened by a cramping pain. That was more than a little kick, she thought.

Billie waddled out of her room and called Hannah. "I think it's time."

"Okay, meet me in the room," said Hannah, and hurried off to get a nurse.

Billie got to the delivery room before anyone else. It was on the second floor, next door to the medical wing where the genetically damaged children were kept. A sort of grim reminder, she swallowed the thought. The room was small, high-ceilinged and dimly lit. A circulating tub sat at one end beside a smart wall. On the other side of the tub, Hannah had setup the Ultra medconsole. Billie started running water in the big tub. Hannah arrived shortly after, with Jorge.

Hannah spoke to a wall panel. "Begin recording. Vertical birth by water. Mother is athletic. Append diagnostics here." She turned back to Billie. "How long since the last . . . " She broke off when Billie's face contorted.

Hannah spoke to the console. "Diagnostic scans. Begin now." She came over and took Billie by the hand. "Here. You had better get your gown on." She glanced at Jorge, who turned away. Hannah monitored the readouts of mother and foetus, heart and brain activity, as Billie changed. Blood pressure, heart rate and oxygen level displays were visible on the console and the wall. When the nurse, Matilda, arrived, Jorge left.

Hannah held Billie's hand again. "Breath deeply," she instructed.

Billie laughed harshly. "I seem to have swallowed something, doctor."

Hannah looked at her and smiled, as tolerant as sin. "Once more. Breathe deeply."

Billie stopped panting and Hannah seemed to be happy with what she saw. She smiled broadly and said, "Okay. Let's get you into the water." She stepped forward and helped Billie down into the pool. The warm water felt good across Billie's back. She felt tight muscles relaxing. Then another contraction wracked her. Matilda held her by the upper arm, while Hannah monitored the readouts above. It burned. In the middle of things, Billie had the strangest impression. Her legs and pelvis were perfectly U shaped and she rang just like a tuning fork. The sound was a baby crying. Then everything turned red.

It was not quite as bad as Billie had heard. She was wracked and sore. What she was not ready for, was the rapture — the rush of sheer joy that enveloped her and carried her far away.

Somehow down at the bottom of the mountain, her body hurt. She could feel her heart still pounding. She hurt. She could feel her bones cracking and rearranging. Hannah held the tiny, tiny girl out to her and all the heavens bowed down and joy made a home in her heart.

Billie took the child in her shaking hands. She had all her fingers and toes. Her head was wreathed in red and black. Just like mom said my hair was, thought Billie. The cord was flattening. The child had stopped crying. She kicked her legs fitfully as Billie held her up.

The child could not perfectly control her mouth and throat, but two shiny bright black eyes tracked Billie's face and the tiny mouth recognizably gargled, "Hello Mother. Xyala sends her greetings."

Extro

"The mythic journey is not across the country; it is into the mind."
— Elgar the Elder, Tau Ceti Colony

✦

THE COMMUNION WAS IN TURMOIL. Xyala had no direct communication with the corporate intelligence, but she could feel the reaction and she heard things from her Liaison. The watery world far behind the giant starship was the reason.

Several aspects of the dominant lifeform had become clear. Humans did not have a useful racial memory. New creatures were born knowing practically nothing and that was almost unimaginable. Further the creatures were alien to each other. Their genetic codes were all slightly different. None of them knew exactly what another was thinking. Evolution had indeed taken an odd turn on that planet.

Such organic isolation had been seen before, but it had always proven nonadaptive. The shipboard Communion had thought the old memories apocryphal, but now they had run headlong into the strangeness, and it was dangerously irrational. The humans killed each other. Genes were destroyed. Capabilities and information were not used or lost — constantly. What was worse, the creatures had destroyed the probe, their only immediate chance of incorporation.

Most peculiar of all, before they had destroyed the probe, the humans had transmitted their life signature — the most intimate and sacrosanct knowledge — through it. The Communion had received and analyzed the genetic data, not knowing what it was at first. As it became clear the data codified millions of different lifeforms, the turmoil had begun. Even as isolated and cut off as Xyala was, she could feel the consternation the situation had engendered.

Lately an even more ominous development had turned up. In the course of studying the humans, Xyala had come across a description of a nanobot dispersion plan called the StarSeed Project. She had duly reported the discovery and had not been surprised when more human radio sources began to be detected nearby.

The Communion on the other hand was convulsed. First there had been one other nearby radio source, then while the Communion had travelled towards it, there were ten, and before long there were a hundred. It was clear the planet behind them had spawned. Human colonies were springing up faster now than a single ship could incorporate them. The turmoil grew proportionally. A new strategy was required. The Communion would withdraw from this region of space to reconsider. Much thought would have to be given the problem, before contact was attempted again.

Elsewhere in the ship, the Communion was busy budding incubator agents to recreate the terran biosphere for study. There were so many separate creatures, they almost needed a planet. Xyala was to continue her studies. She had much of the historical data yet to analyze and her discoveries had proven their worth.

Xyala was watching, as she did frequently, the human in body armour approach her probe. The wall-sized video display she was watching blinked and she was informed the Liaison was approaching. Xyala froze the playback and looked up as her contact entered her workspace.

"There is another one," the Liaison said without preamble.

Xyala nodded and then, realizing this reaction meant nothing to her contact, said, "Why am I not surprised?" The human radio sources were popping up on star systems all around the planet. She had projected the number of systems the humans would occupy simply following the trend line and been vaguely amused. The Communion had met a formidable competitor.

The Liaison looked at the frozen image of Billie on the moon. "Are the creatures understood?"

"No. Not really. I have to study for kilochrons to gain an inkling of the beginnings of an idea of what they really are. It may be there are some chasms we never cross."

The Liaison jerked reflexively in a pattern which meant she did not understand. "The HCA speaks more and more like one of them. The idiosyncratic speech quotient is rising steadily."

Xyala did not reply. She knew better than to try to lead her contact where she would not go. "Some chasms we may never cross" indeed. She wondered what a human would think of the discussion.

When the Liaison left, Xyala finished playing the recording of the human and the probe once more. The probe machine was engulfing the legs of the suit, analyzing the structure and probing to reach the creature inside. Then the human unexpectedly opened the suit. The last message said, "Contact initiated," but then the human dropped the destructive crystal and the link was broken.

What had happened to the probe, Xyala wondered. What had happened to the human? In the decision tree she had designed for the probe, if in danger and unable to complete the primary mission, the priority was to initiate long term contact, but Xyala did not know what had happened. She turned from her console and walked across the room to the wall-sized, realtime display of space behind the ship.

Xyala held a pseudopod between her eye and the tiny dot of the distant star. The planet had long since ceased to be visible. What was that human nursery rhyme she had recorded?

"Star light, star bright,
First star I see tonight,
I wish I may, I wish I might,
Have the wish I wish tonight."

And what shall I wish for, she wondered, what shall I wish for?

ABOUT THE AUTHOR

Water is H.E. TAYLOR's first novel. He lives in Winnipeg where he works as a computer programmer and writer.